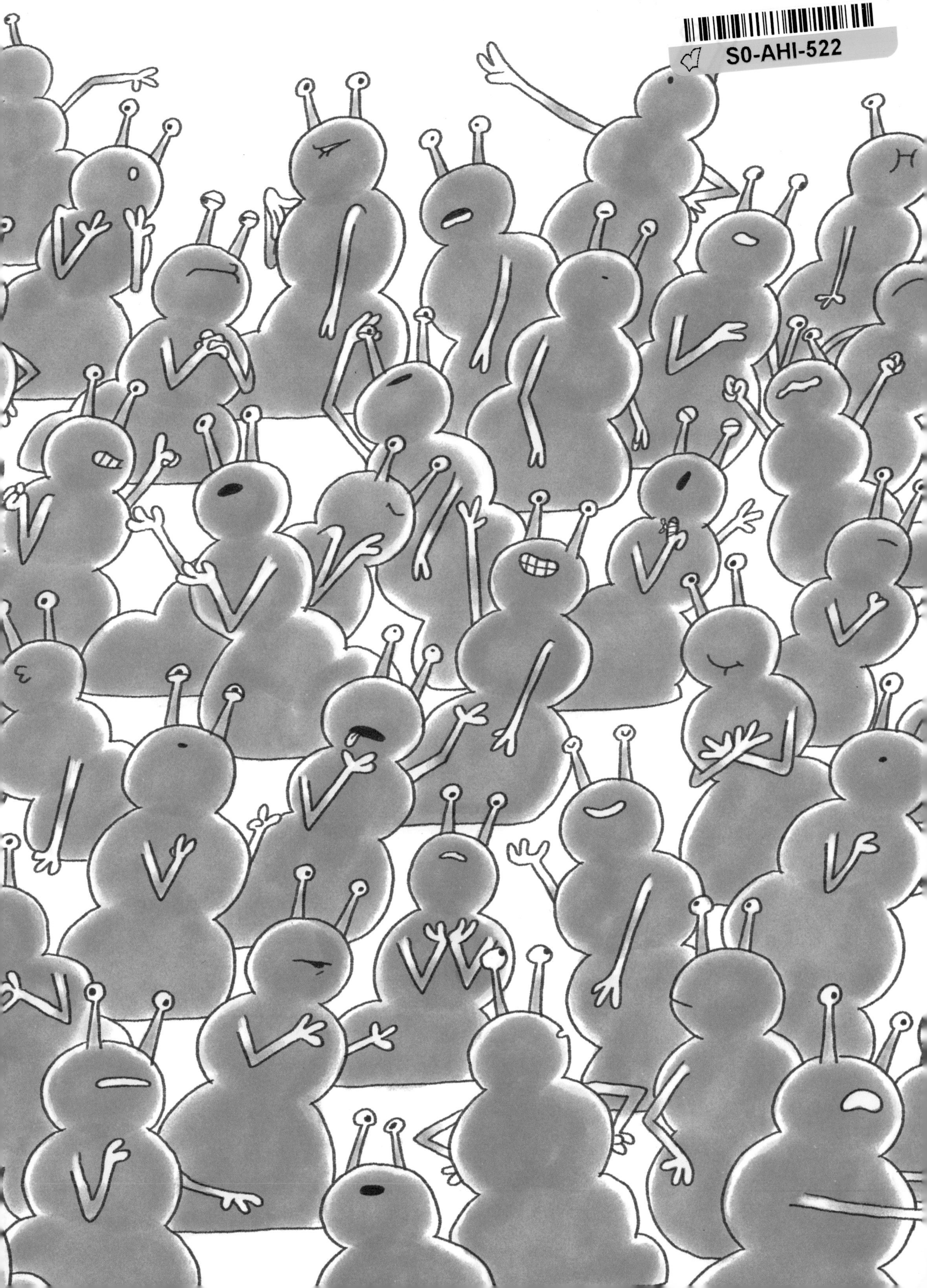

This Is **NOT** My Story

For Patrick L. Here's wishing you a lifetime filled with great stories! — R.U.

For the FFs, whose storytelling takes me to other worlds, through time and across dimensions — D.H.

Text © 2023 Ryan Uytdewilligen
Illustrations © 2023 David Huyck

Published in Canada and the U.S. by Kids Can Press Ltd.
25 Dockside Drive, Toronto, ON M5A 0B5

Kids Can Press is a Corus Entertainment Inc. company

www.kidscanpress.com

The artwork in this book was rendered with electrons traveling at unimaginable speeds, using a trusty Stumpy Pencil digital brush and other feats of modern technological magic.

The text is set in Zack and Sarah, Vision, and Wellfleet.

Edited by Jennifer Stokes and Olga Kidisevic
Designed by Marie Bartholomew

Printed and bound in Buji, Shenzhen, China, in 10/2022 by WKT Company

CM 23 0 9 8 7 6 5 4 3 2 1

Library and Archives Canada Cataloguing in Publication

Title: This is not my story / written by Ryan Uytdewilligen ; illustrated by David Huyck.
Names: Uytdewilligen, Ryan, 1992– author. | Huyck, David, 1976– illustrator.
Identifiers: Canadiana 20220224587 | ISBN 9781525303432 (hardcover)
Classification: LCC PS8641.Y83 T55 2023 | DDC jC813/.6 — dc23

Kids Can Press gratefully acknowledges that the land on which our office is located is the traditional territory of many nations, including the Mississaugas of the Credit, the Anishnabeg, the Chippewa, the Haudenosaunee and the Wendat peoples, and is now home to many diverse First Nations, Inuit and Métis peoples.

We thank the Government of Ontario, through Ontario Creates; the Ontario Arts Council; the Canada Council for the Arts; and the Government of Canada for supporting our publishing activity.

This Is NOT My Story

Written by Ryan Uytdewilligen

Illustrated by David Huyck

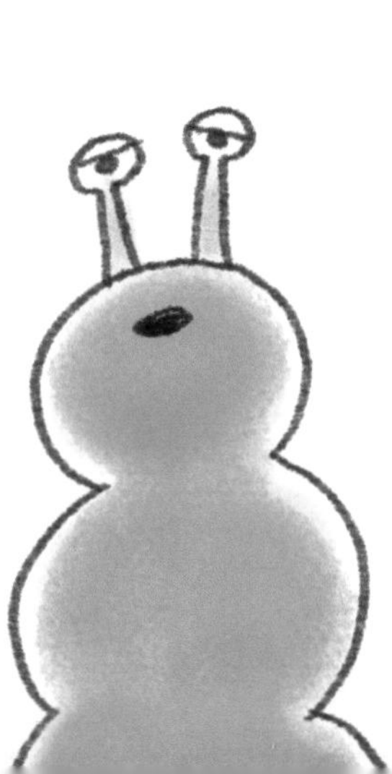

Kids Can Press

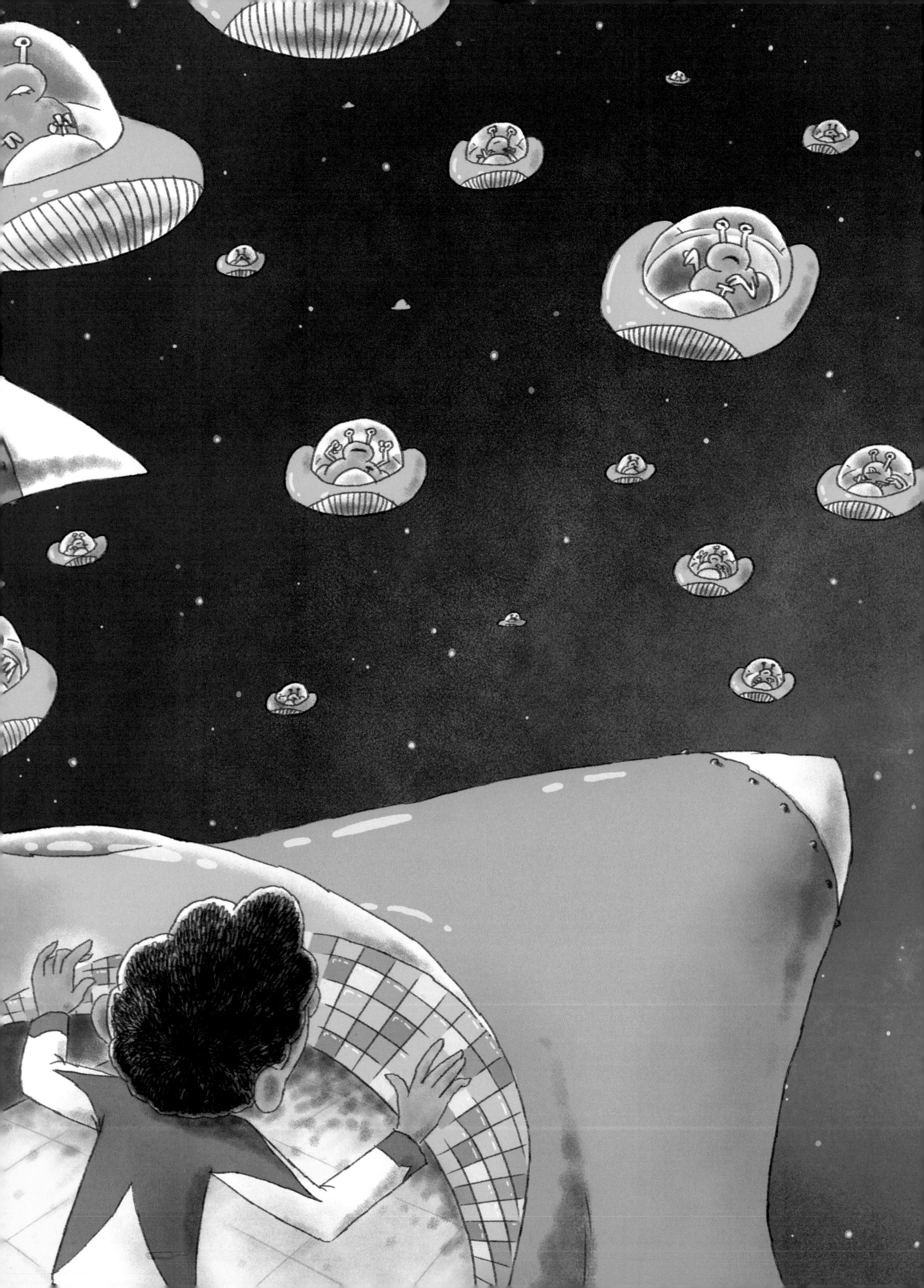

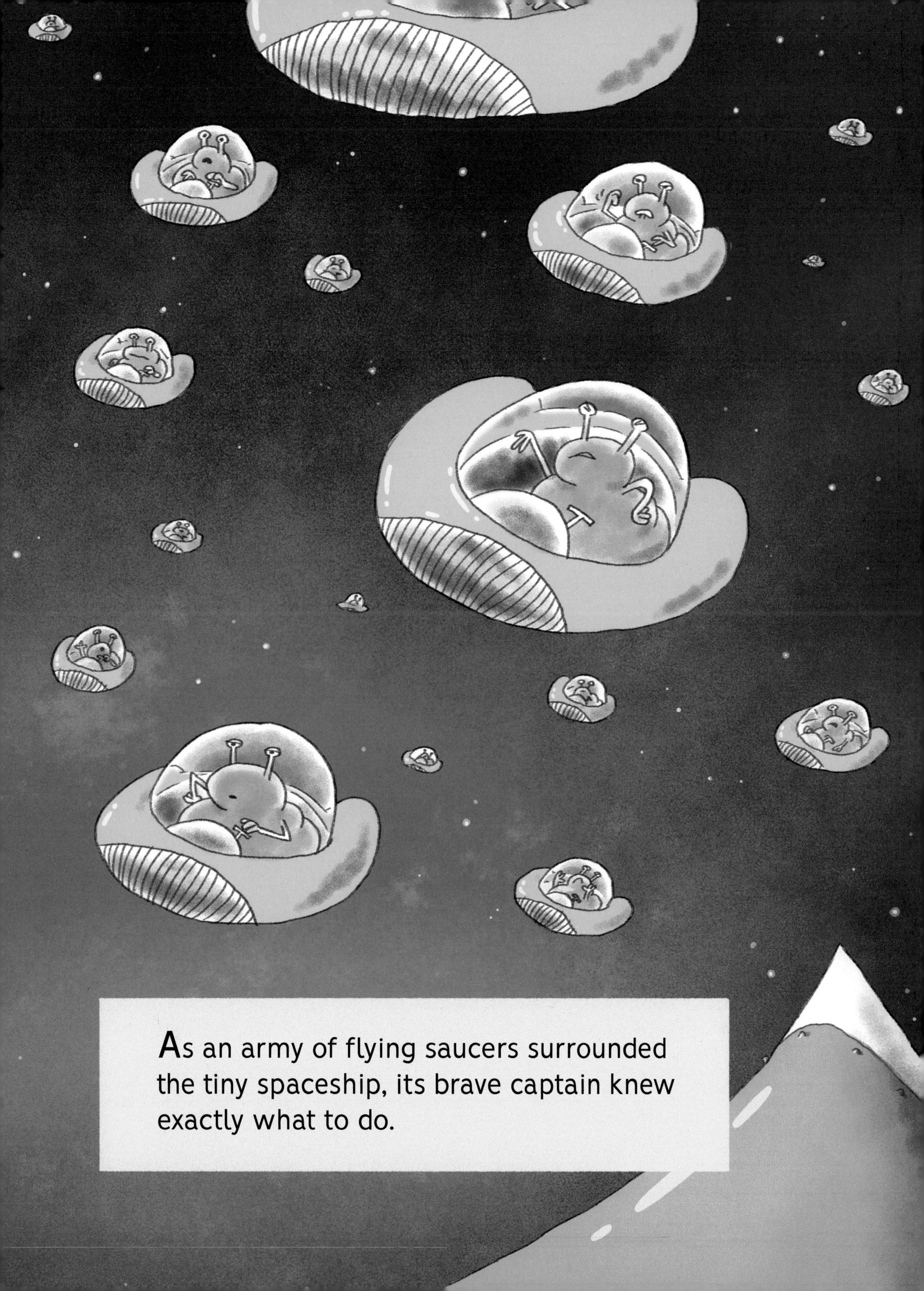

As an army of flying saucers surrounded the tiny spaceship, its brave captain knew exactly what to do.

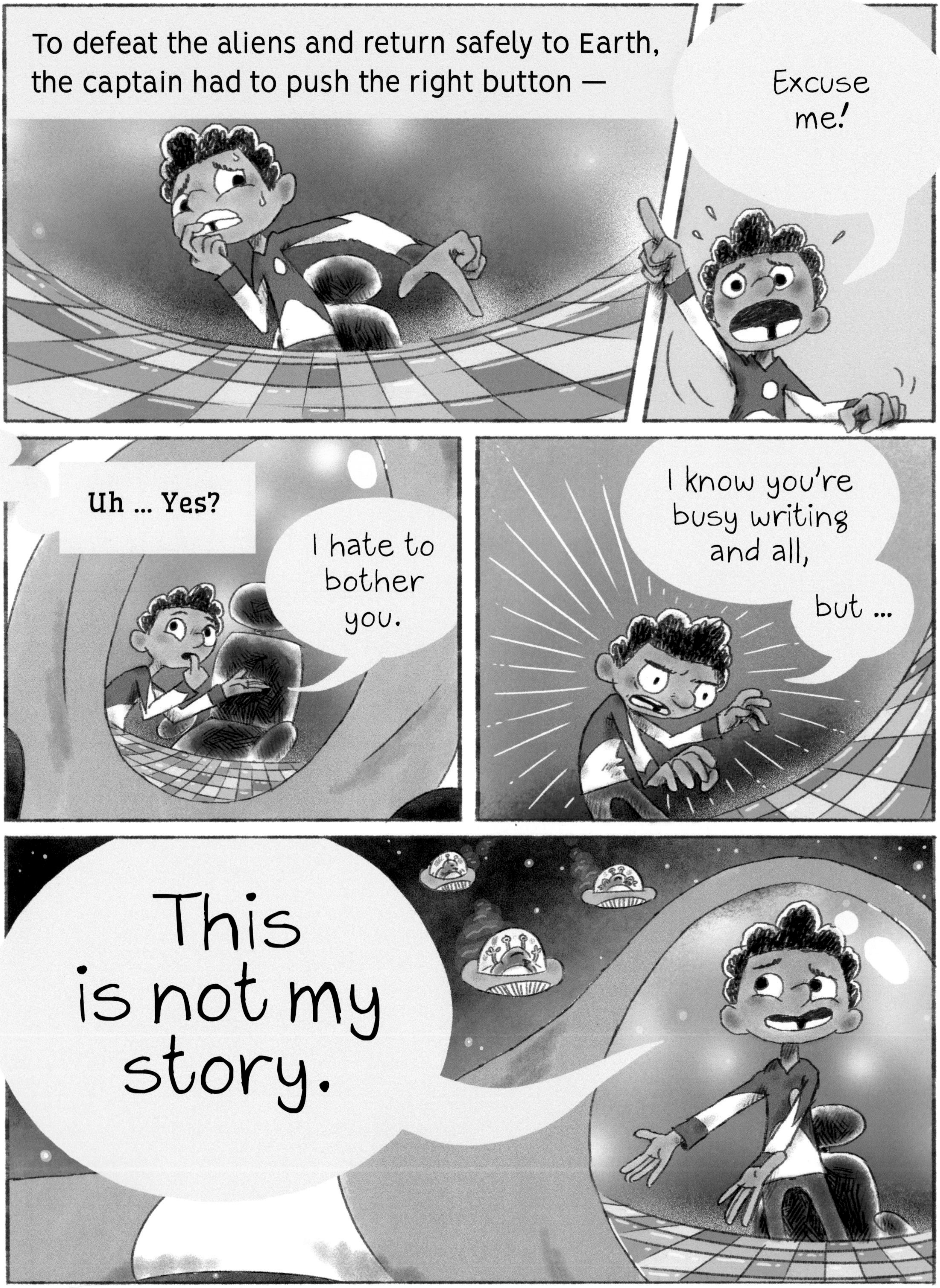
To defeat the aliens and return safely to Earth, the captain had to push the right button —
Excuse me!
Uh ... Yes?
I hate to bother you.
I know you're busy writing and all,
but ...
This is not my story.

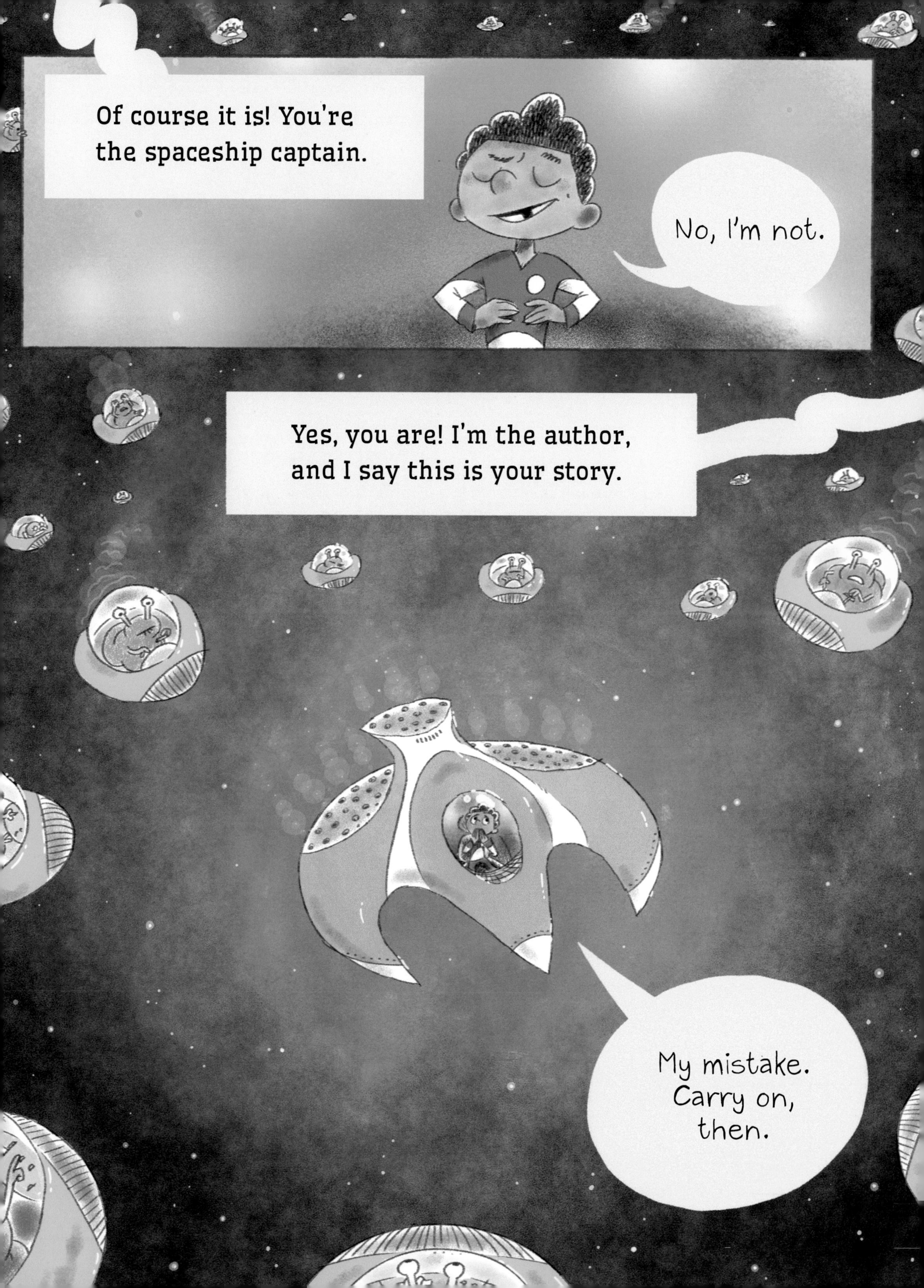
Of course it is! You're the spaceship captain.
No, I'm not.
Yes, you are! I'm the author, and I say this is your story.
My mistake. Carry on, then.

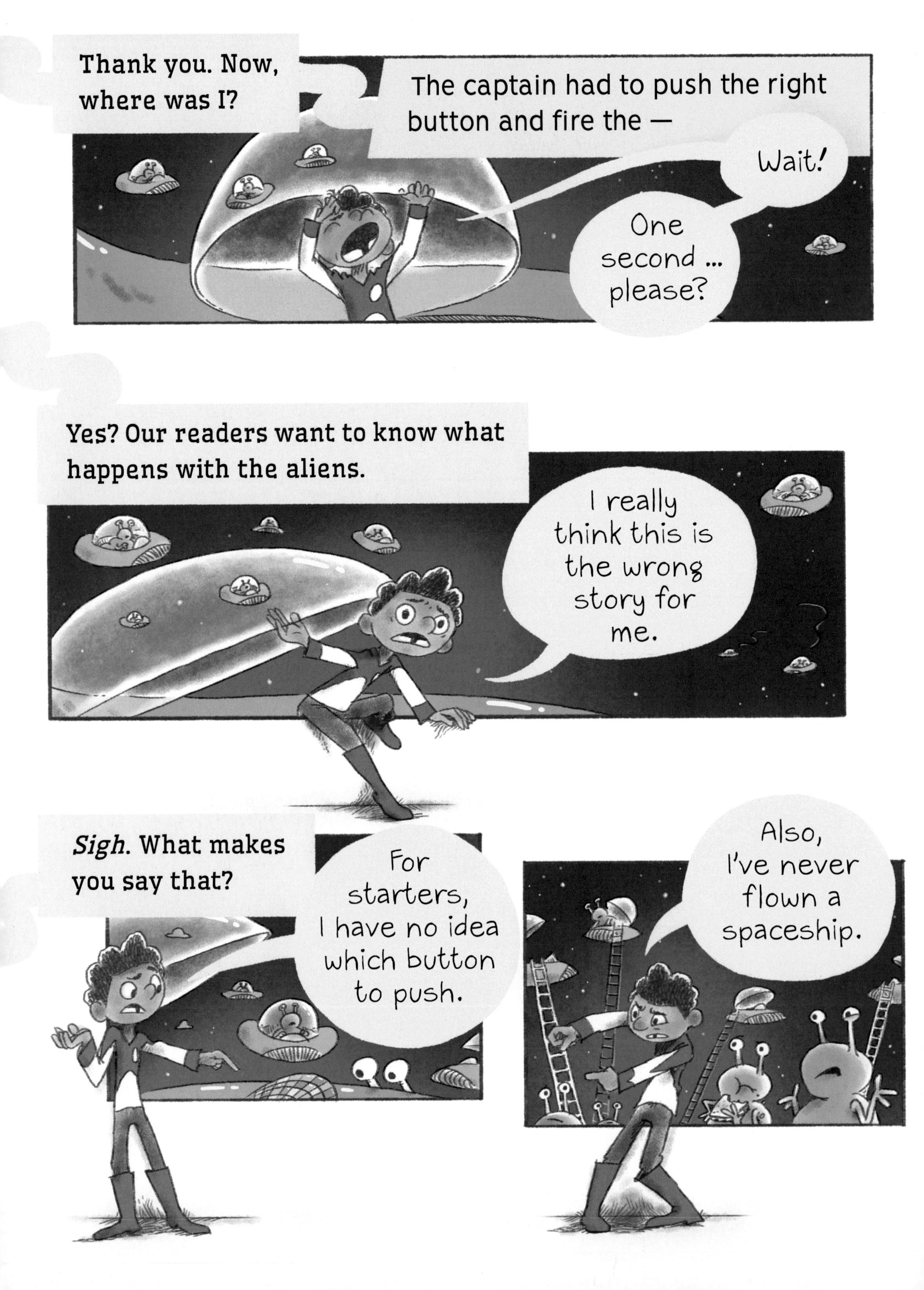

Thank you. Now, where was I?
The captain had to push the right button and fire the —
Wait!
One second ... please?
Yes? Our readers want to know what happens with the aliens.
I really think this is the wrong story for me.
Sigh. What makes you say that?
For starters, I have no idea which button to push.
Also, I've never flown a spaceship.

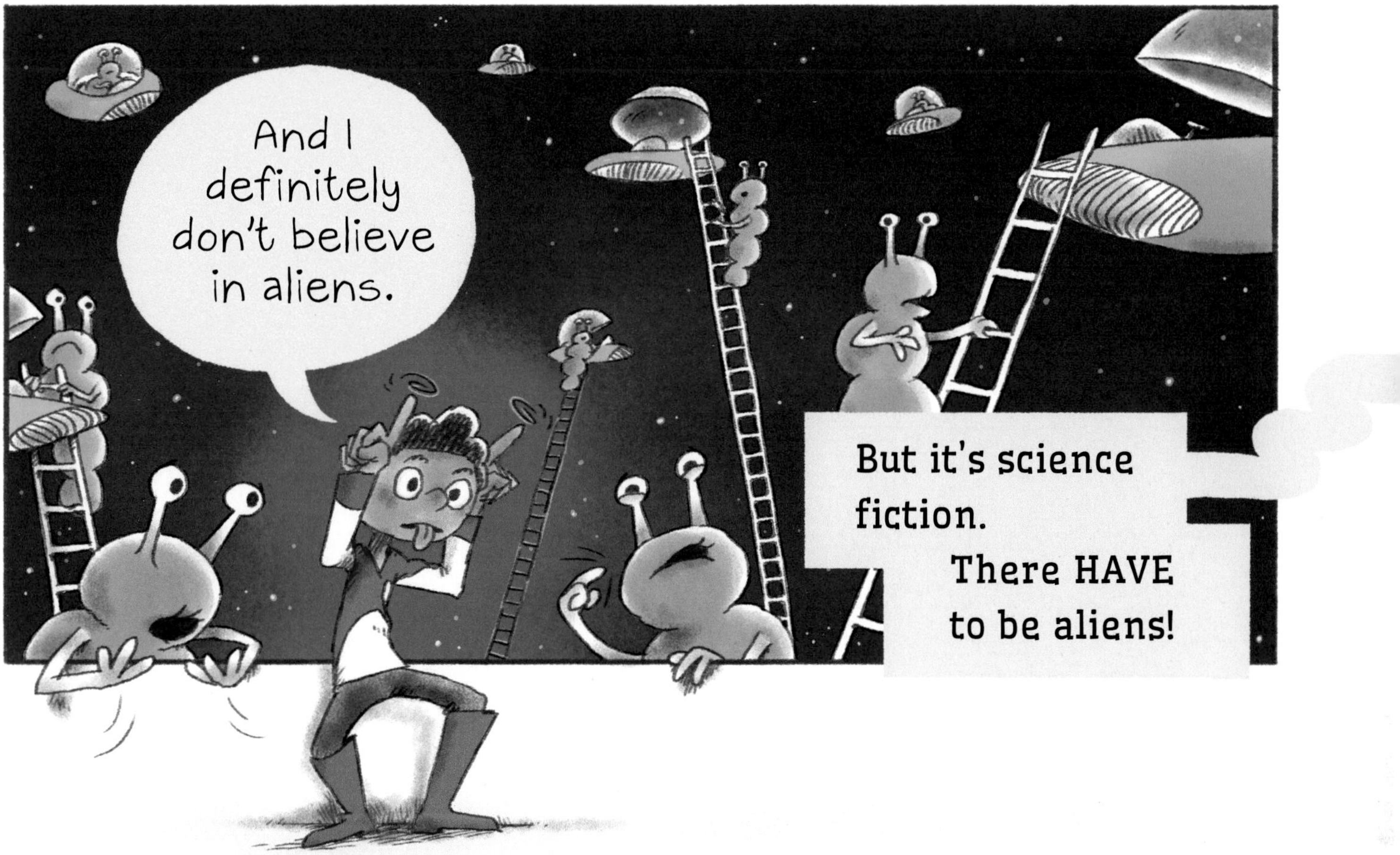
And I definitely don't believe in aliens.
But it's science fiction.
There HAVE to be aliens!

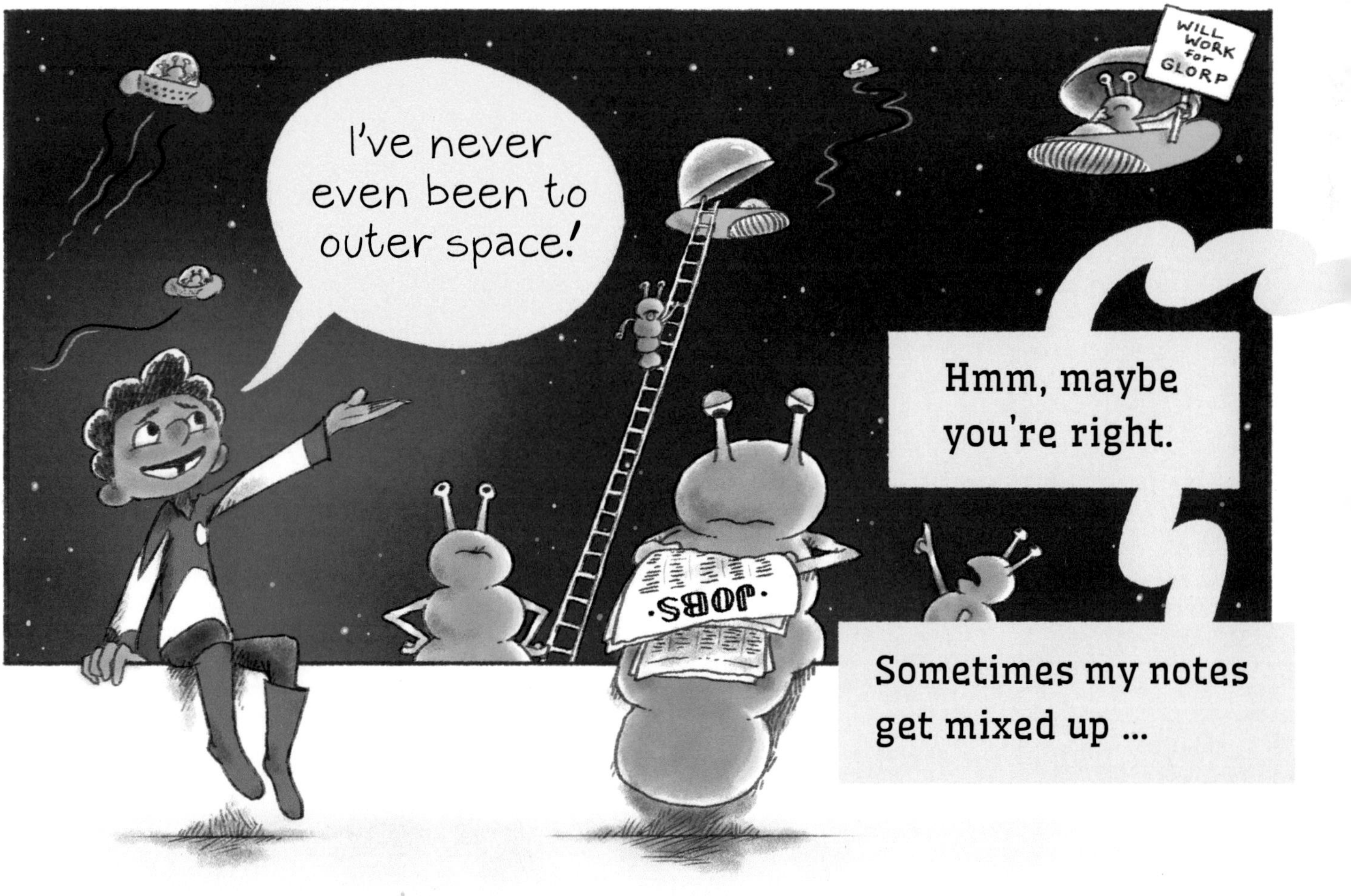
WILL WORK for GLORP
I've never even been to outer space!
Hmm, maybe you're right.
Sometimes my notes get mixed up ...

Let's find out which story
you're supposed to be in.

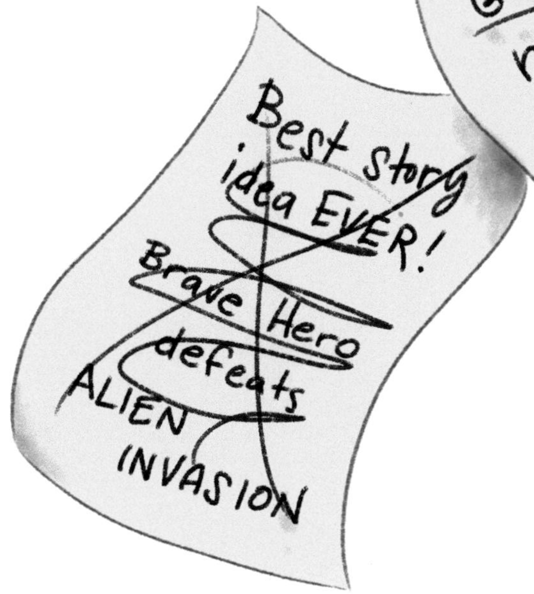
Best story idea EVER!
Brave Hero defeats ALIEN INVASION

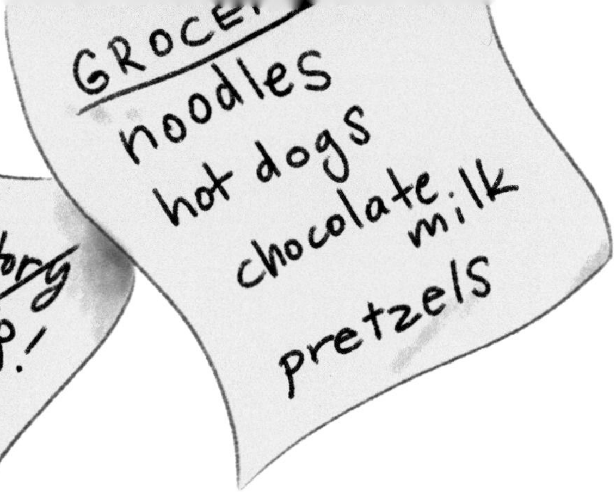
GROCE
noodles
hot dogs
chocolate milk
pretzels

Ah! Here we are ...

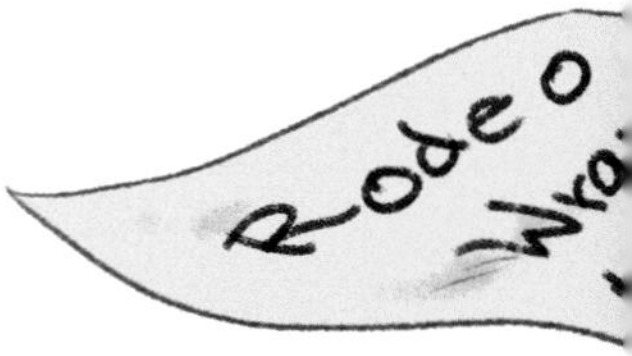
Rodeo

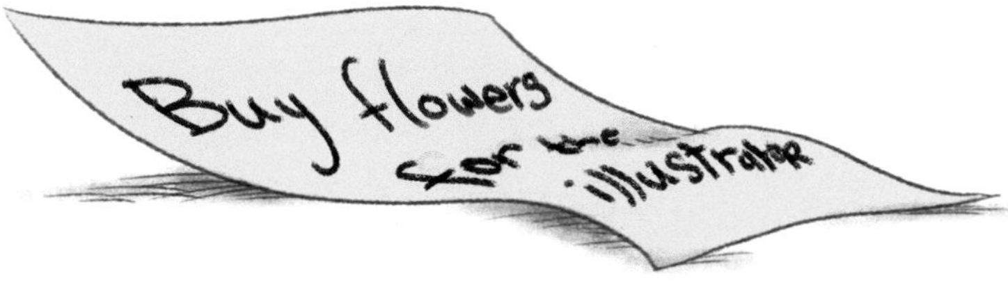
Buy flowers for the illustrator

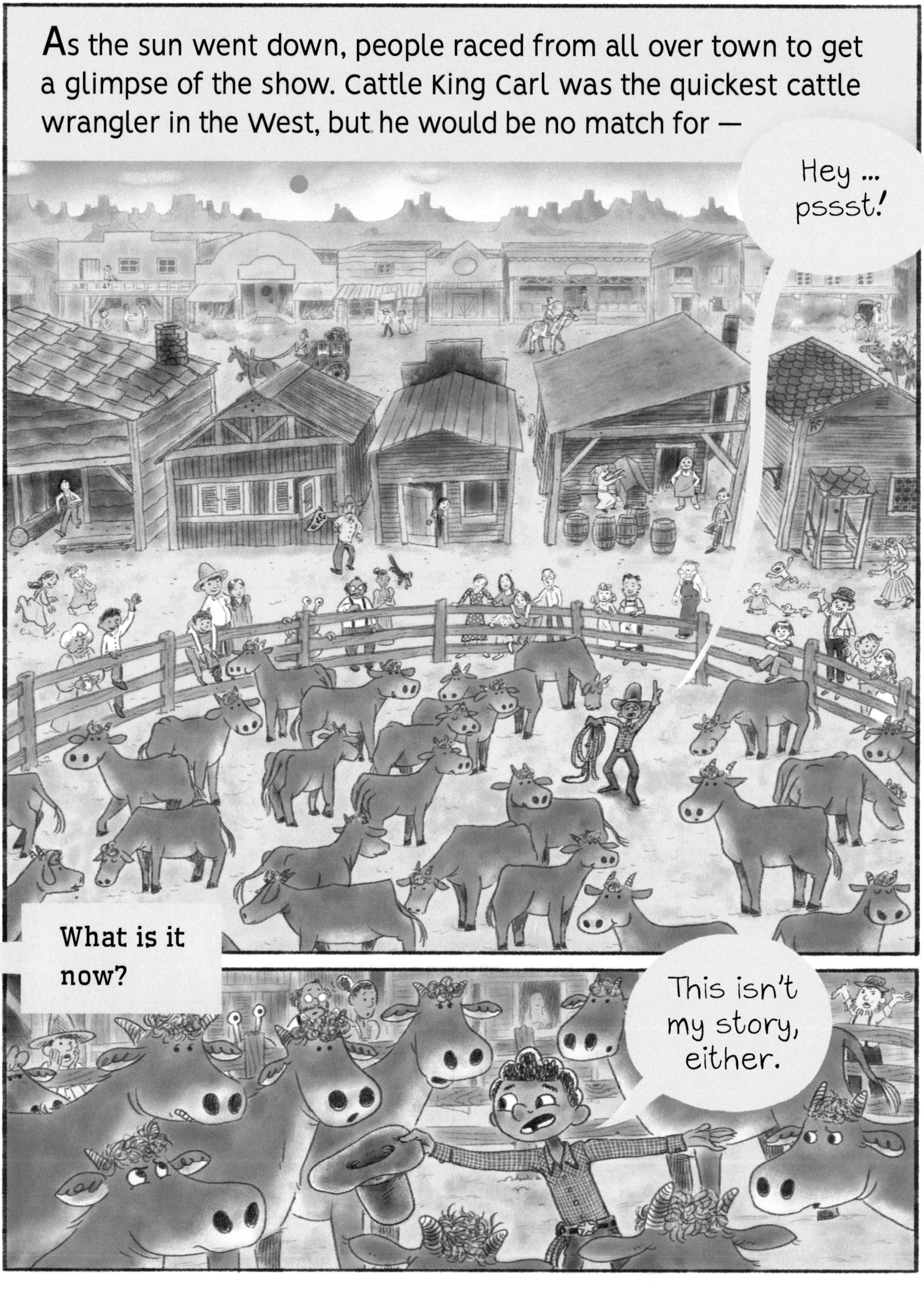
As the sun went down, people raced from all over town to get a glimpse of the show. Cattle King Carl was the quickest cattle wrangler in the West, but he would be no match for —
Hey ... pssst!
What is it now?
This isn't my story, either.

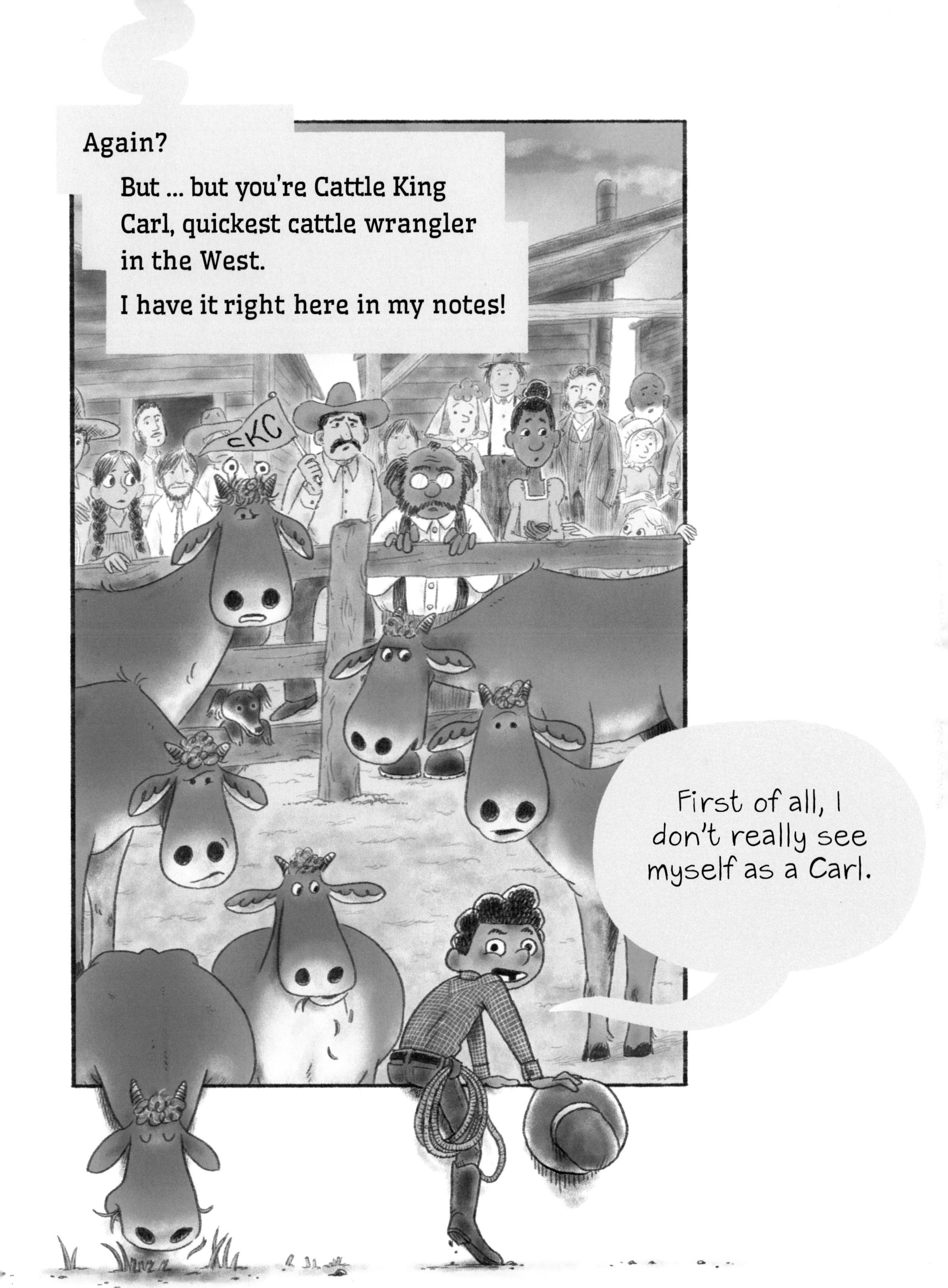
Again?
But ... but you're Cattle King Carl, quickest cattle wrangler in the West.
I have it right here in my notes!
CKC
First of all, I don't really see myself as a Carl.

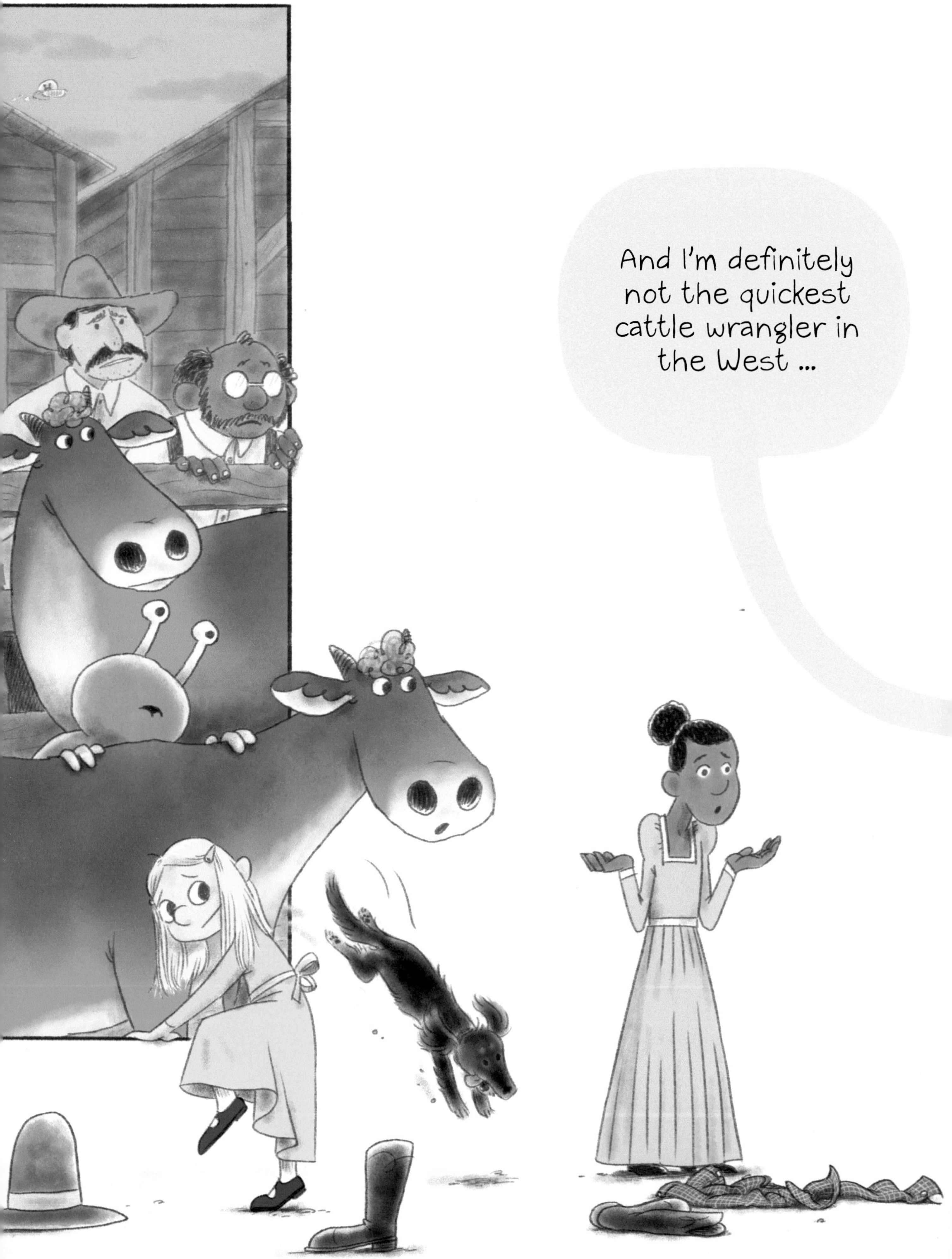
And I'm definitely not the quickest cattle wrangler in the West ...

Or the East,

South

or North,

for that matter.

Fine, hold on ...

Once upon a time, a valiant dragon-slaying knight protected a mighty kingdom. But when the most dangerous, most frightening, most spine-tingling —

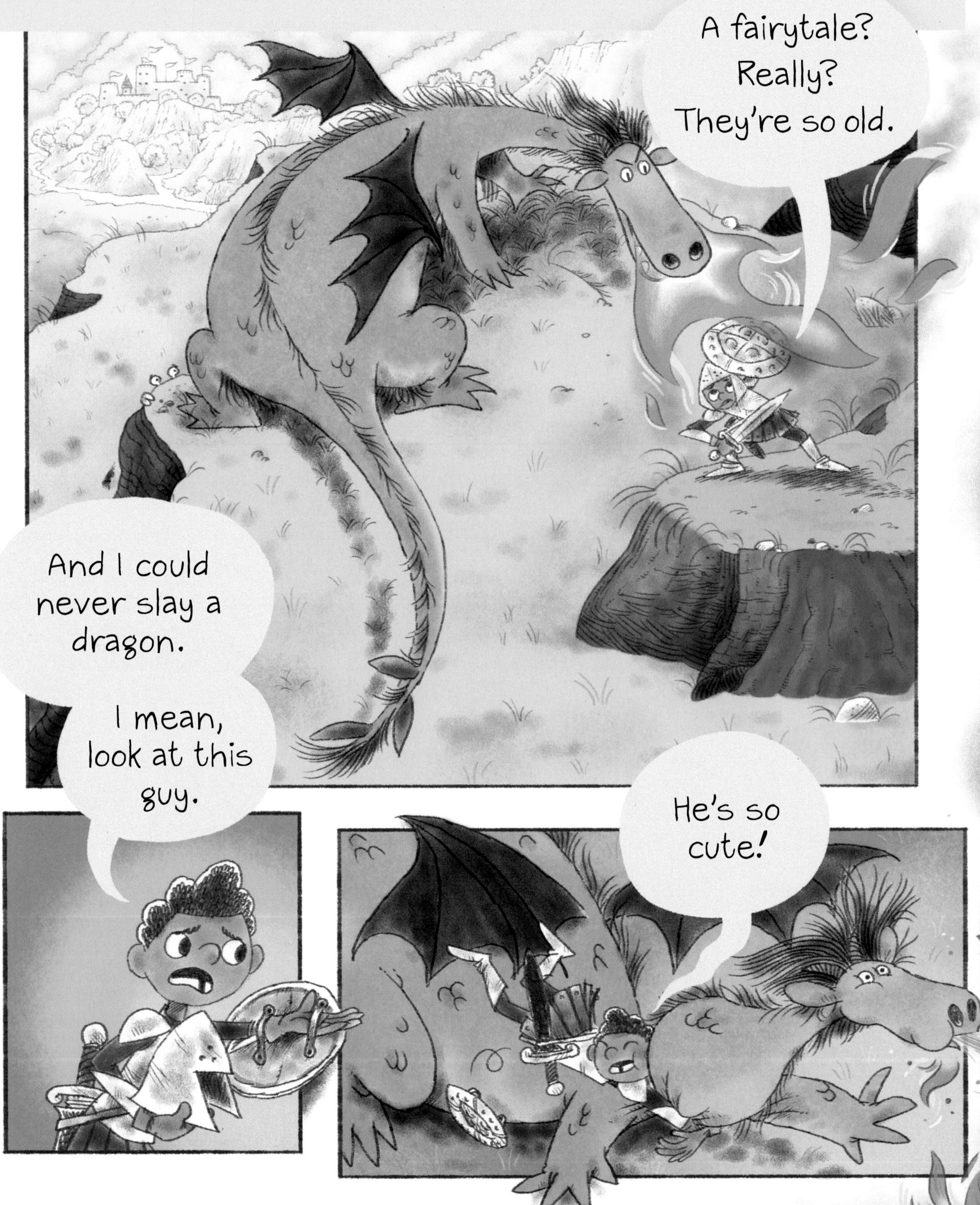
A fairytale? Really? They're so old.
And I could never slay a dragon.
I mean, look at this guy.
He's so cute!

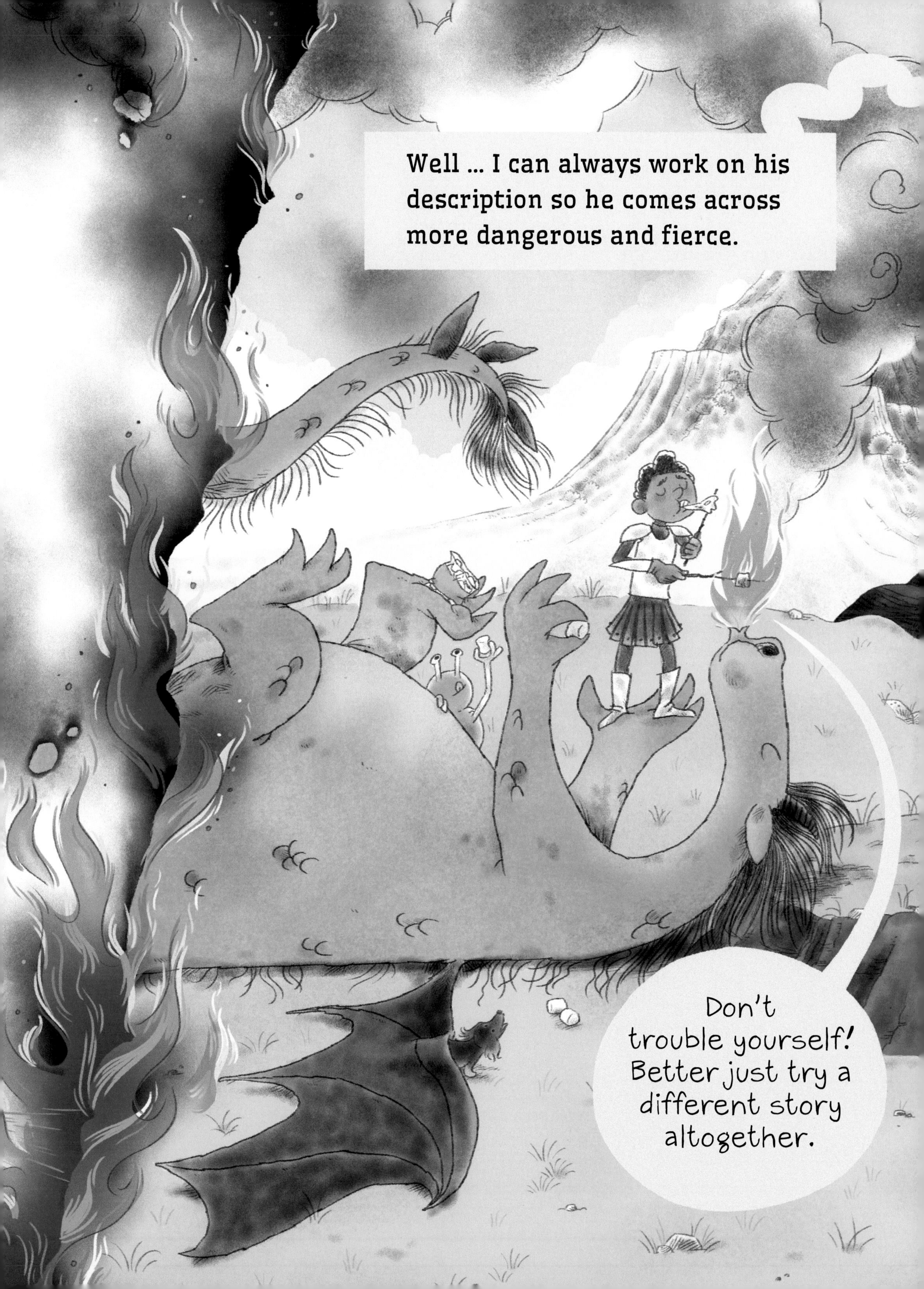
Well ... I can always work on his description so he comes across more dangerous and fierce.
Don't trouble yourself! Better just try a different story altogether.

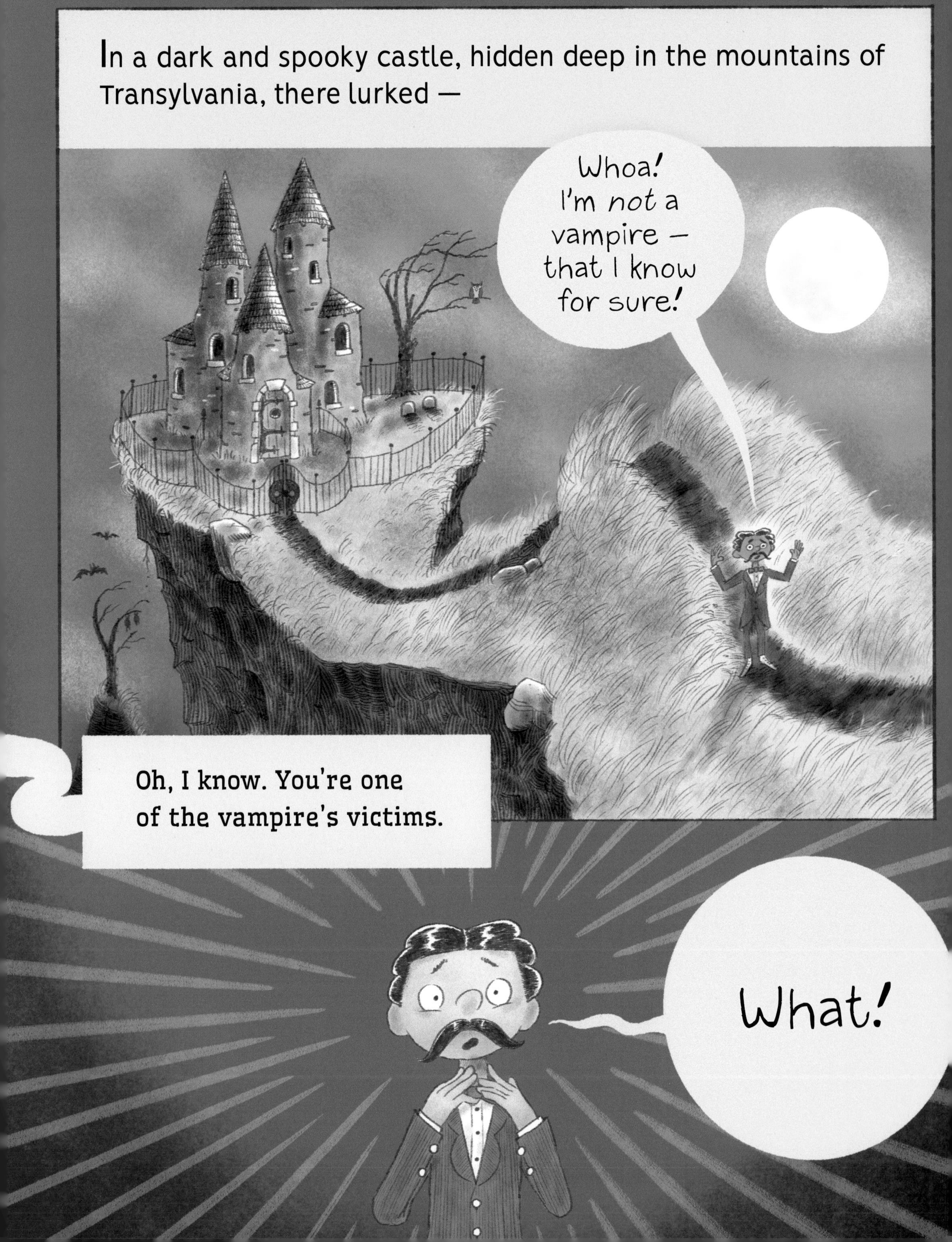
In a dark and spooky castle, hidden deep in the mountains of Transylvania, there lurked —
Whoa! I'm *not* a vampire — that I know for sure!
Oh, I know. You're one of the vampire's victims.
What!

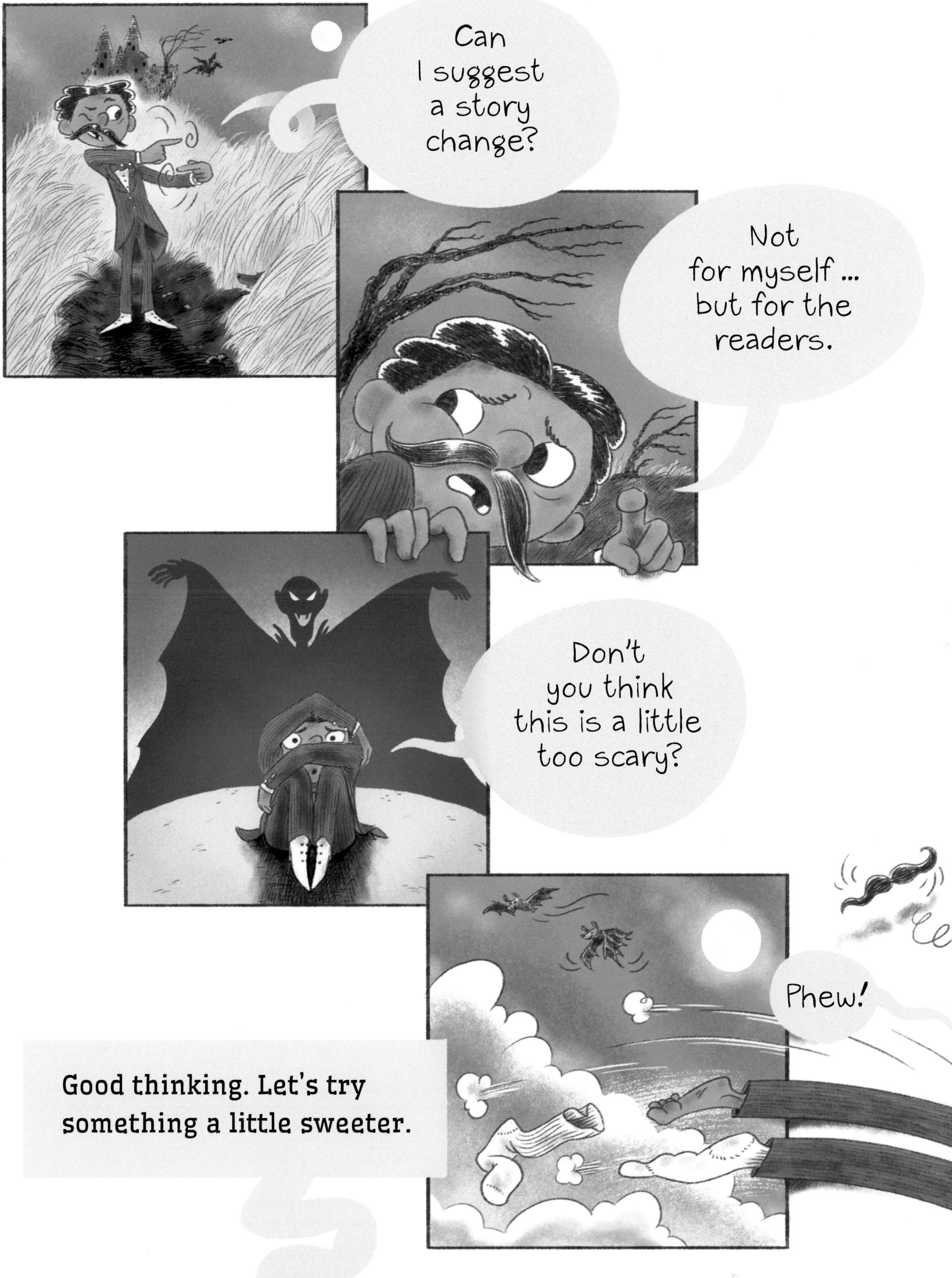
Can I suggest a story change?
Not for myself ... but for the readers.
Don't you think this is a little too scary?
Phew!
Good thinking. Let's try something a little sweeter.

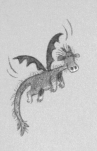

It was a crisp autumn morning in Paris, and Pierre, flowers in hand —

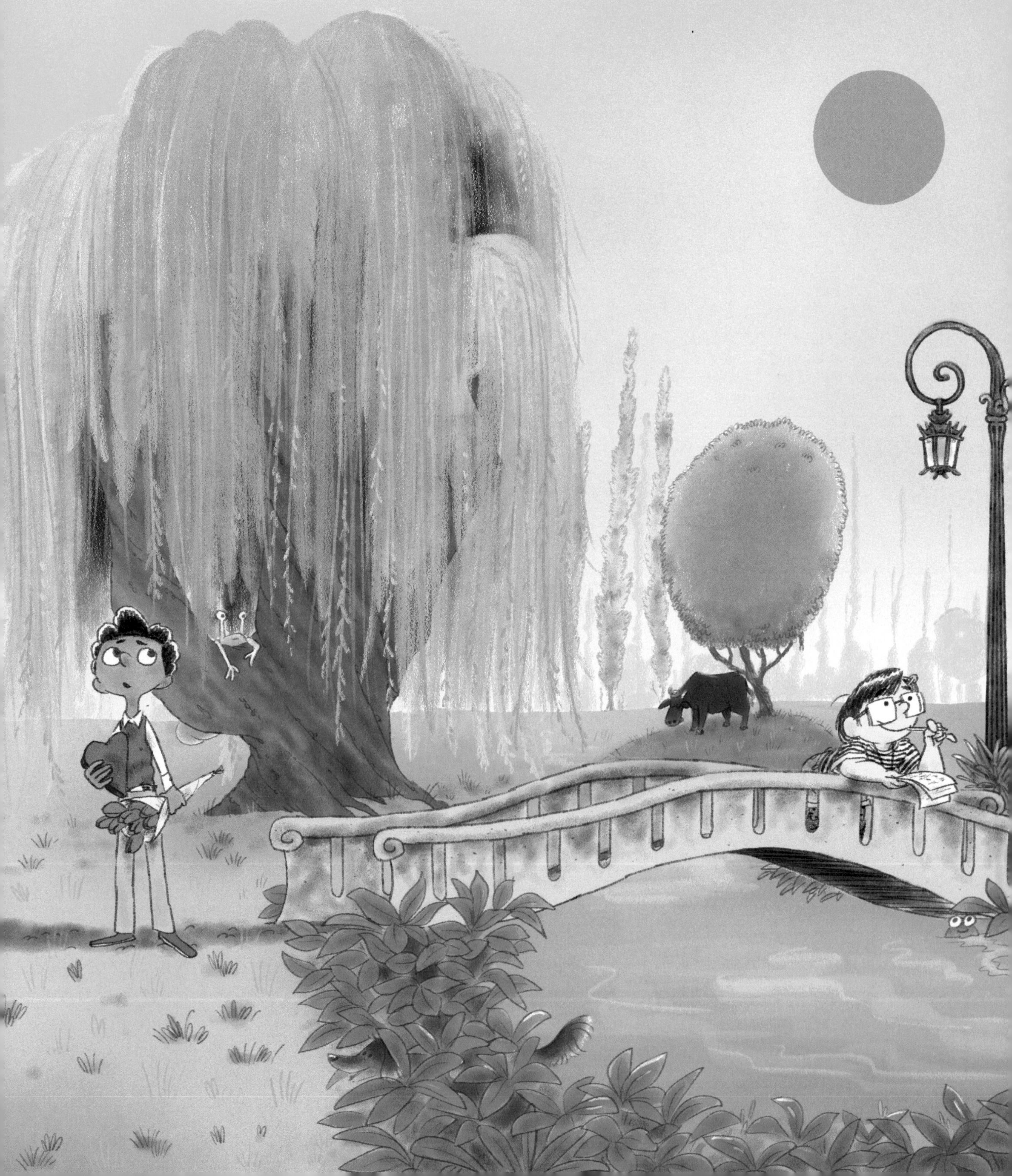

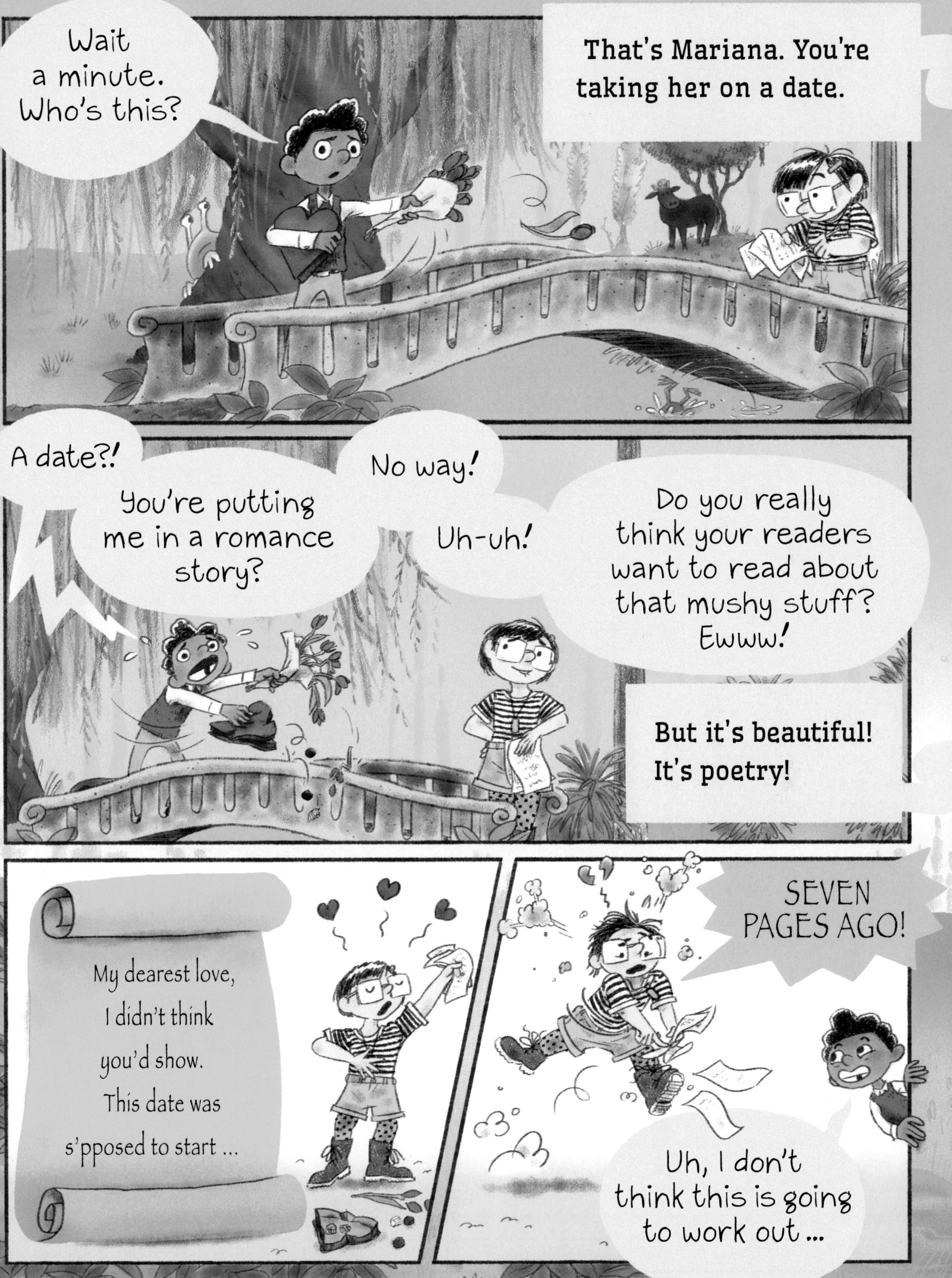
Wait a minute. Who's this?
That's Mariana. You're taking her on a date.
A date?!
No way!
You're putting me in a romance story?
Uh-uh!
Do you really think your readers want to read about that mushy stuff? Ewww!
But it's beautiful! It's poetry!
My dearest love,
I didn't think
you'd show.
This date was
s'pposed to start ...
SEVEN PAGES AGO!
Uh, I don't think this is going to work out ...

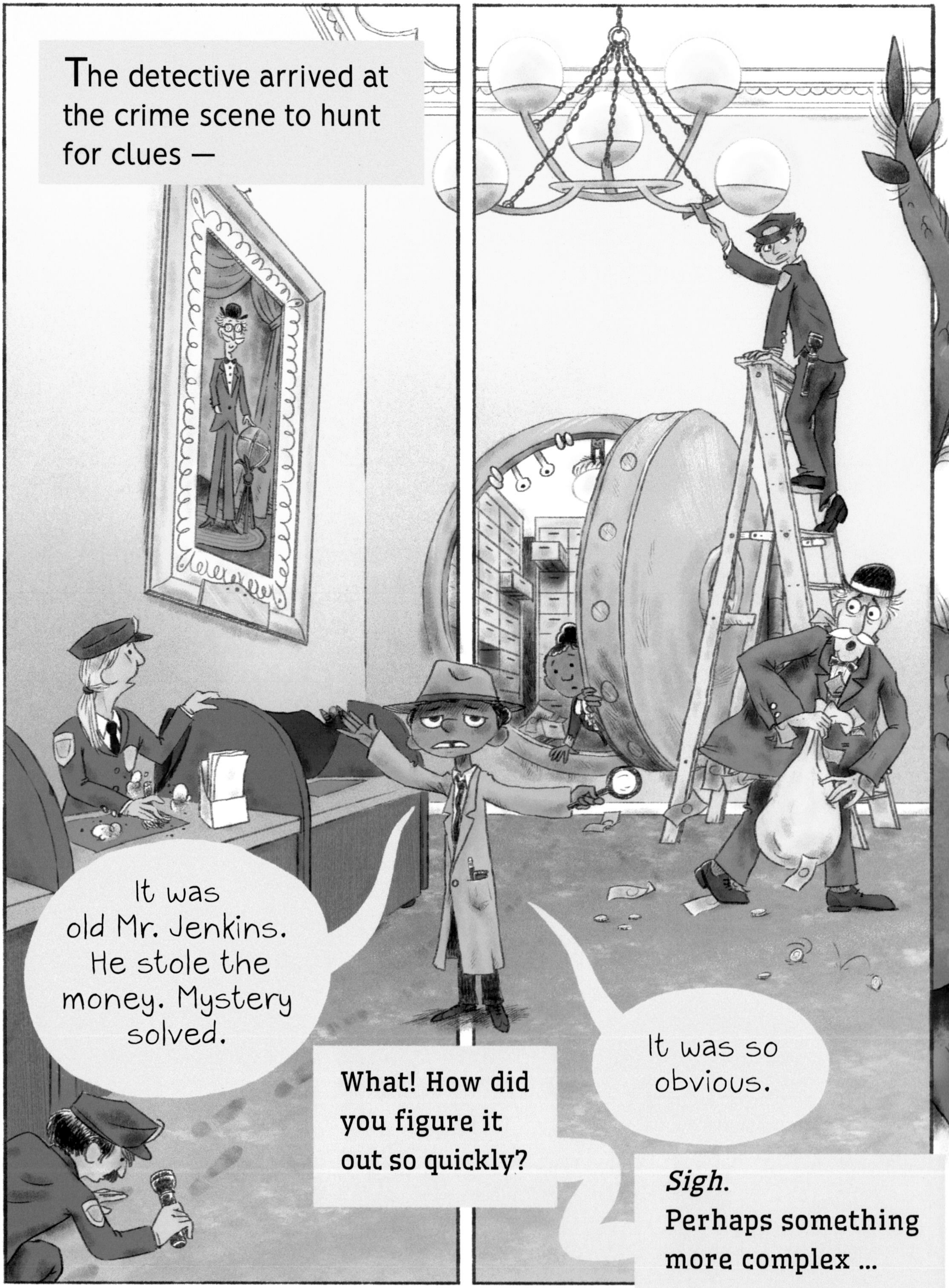
The detective arrived at the crime scene to hunt for clues —
It was old Mr. Jenkins. He stole the money. Mystery solved.
What! How did you figure it out so quickly?
It was so obvious.
Sigh.
Perhaps something more complex ...

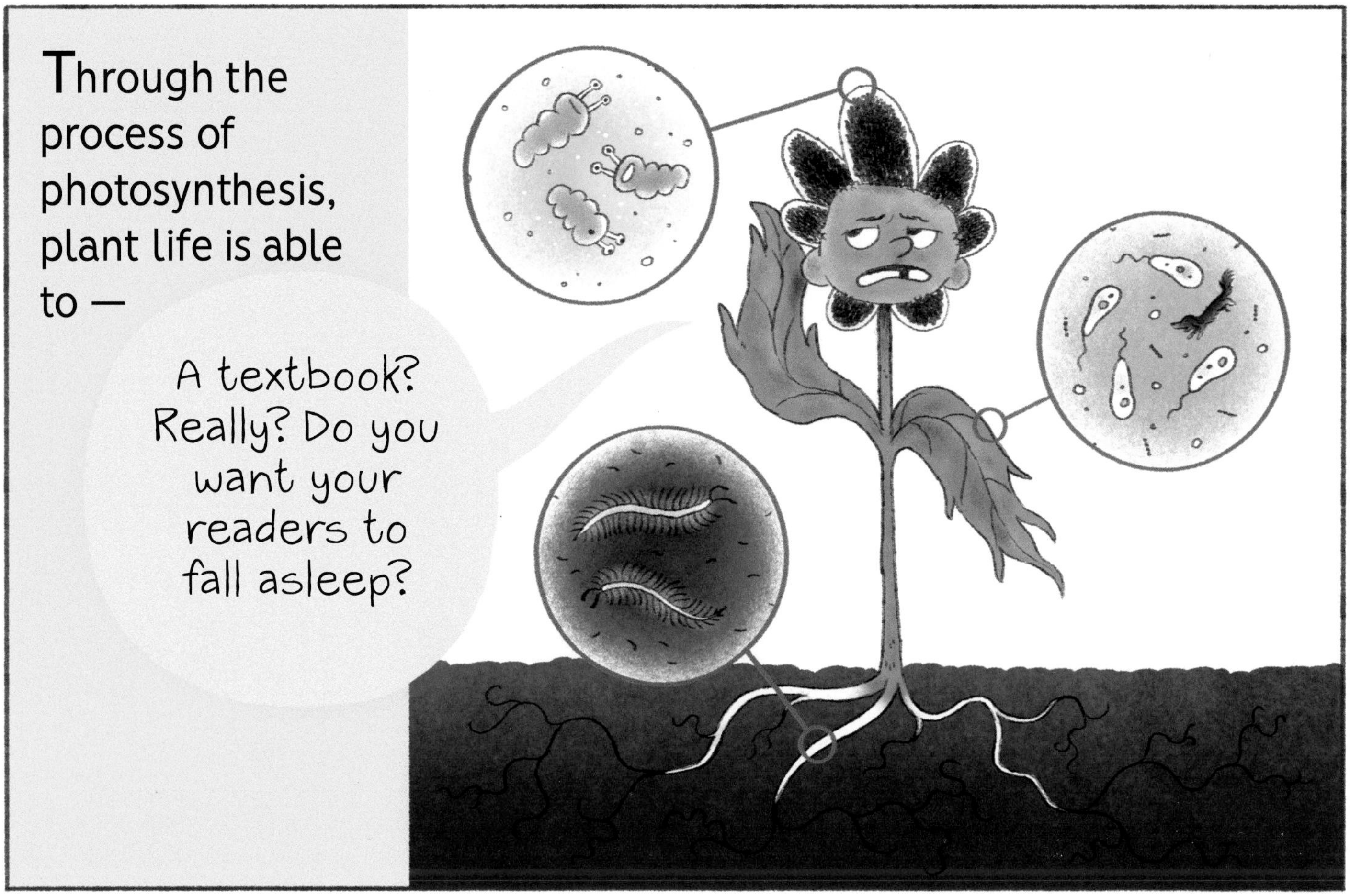
Through the process of photosynthesis, plant life is able to —
A textbook? Really? Do you want your readers to fall asleep?

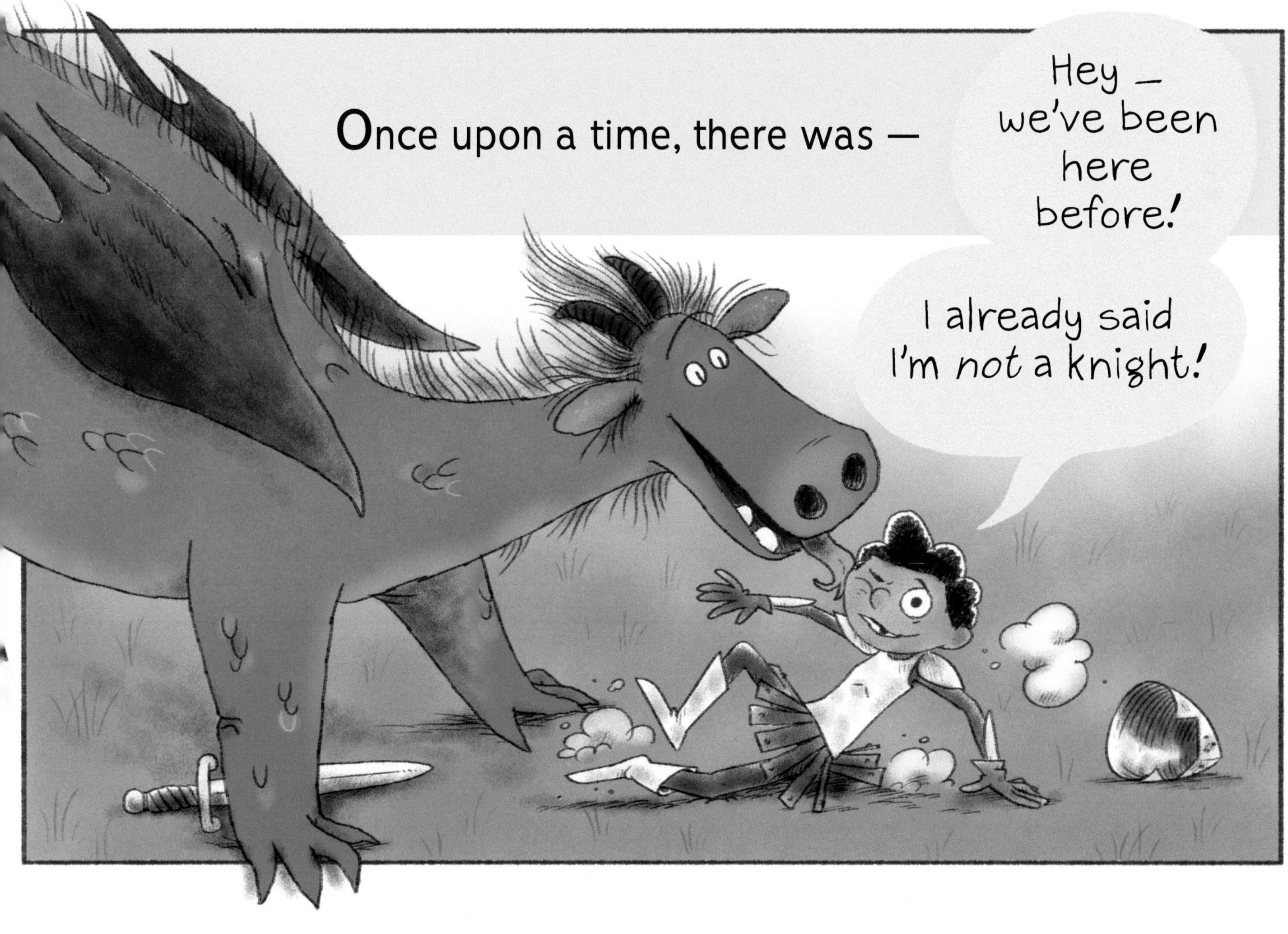
Once upon a time, there was —
Hey — we've been here before!
I already said I'm *not* a knight!

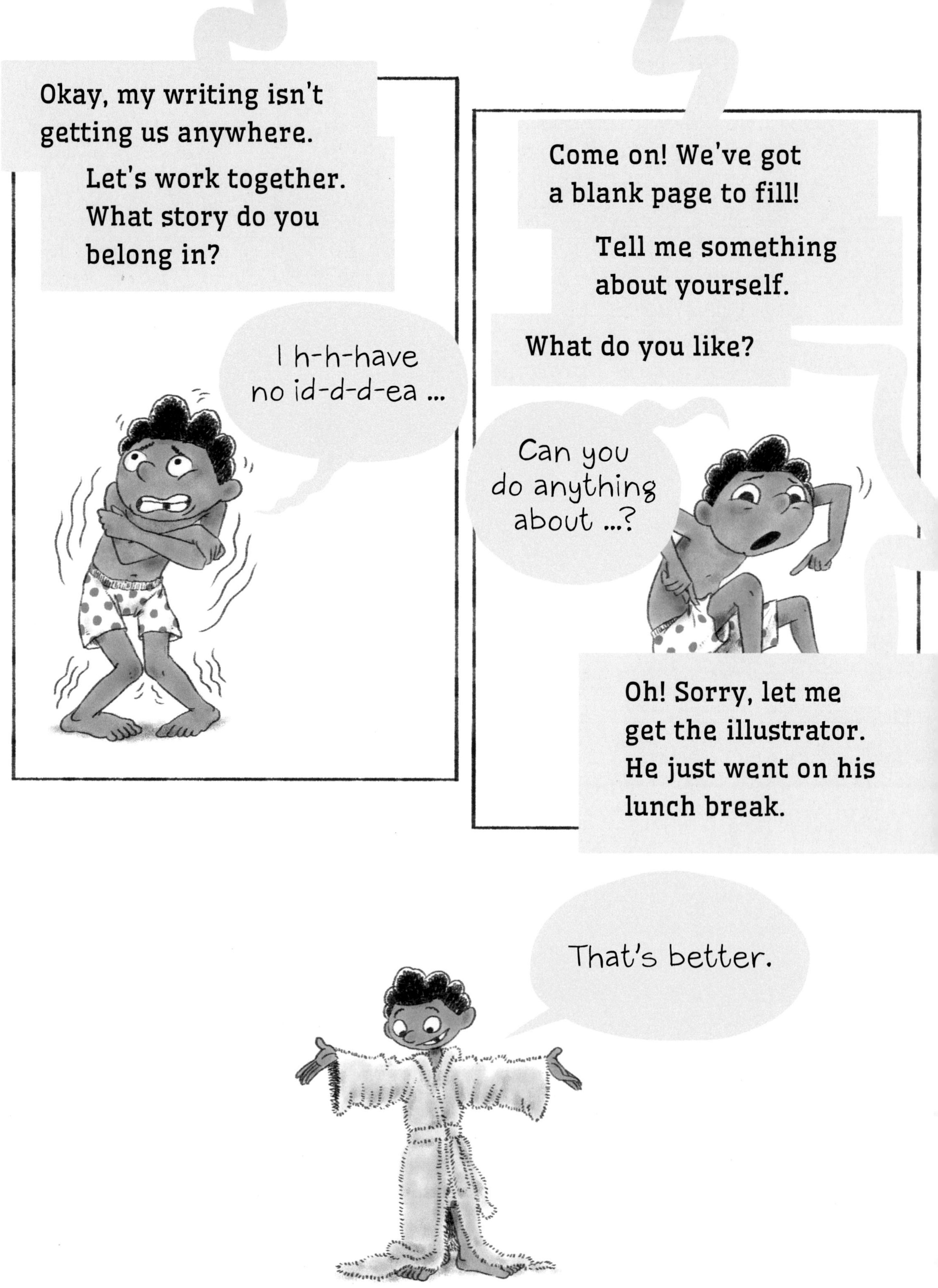
Okay, my writing isn't getting us anywhere.
Let's work together. What story do you belong in?
I h-h-have no id-d-d-ea ...
Come on! We've got a blank page to fill!
Tell me something about yourself.
What do you like?
Can you do anything about ...?
Oh! Sorry, let me get the illustrator. He just went on his lunch break.
That's better.

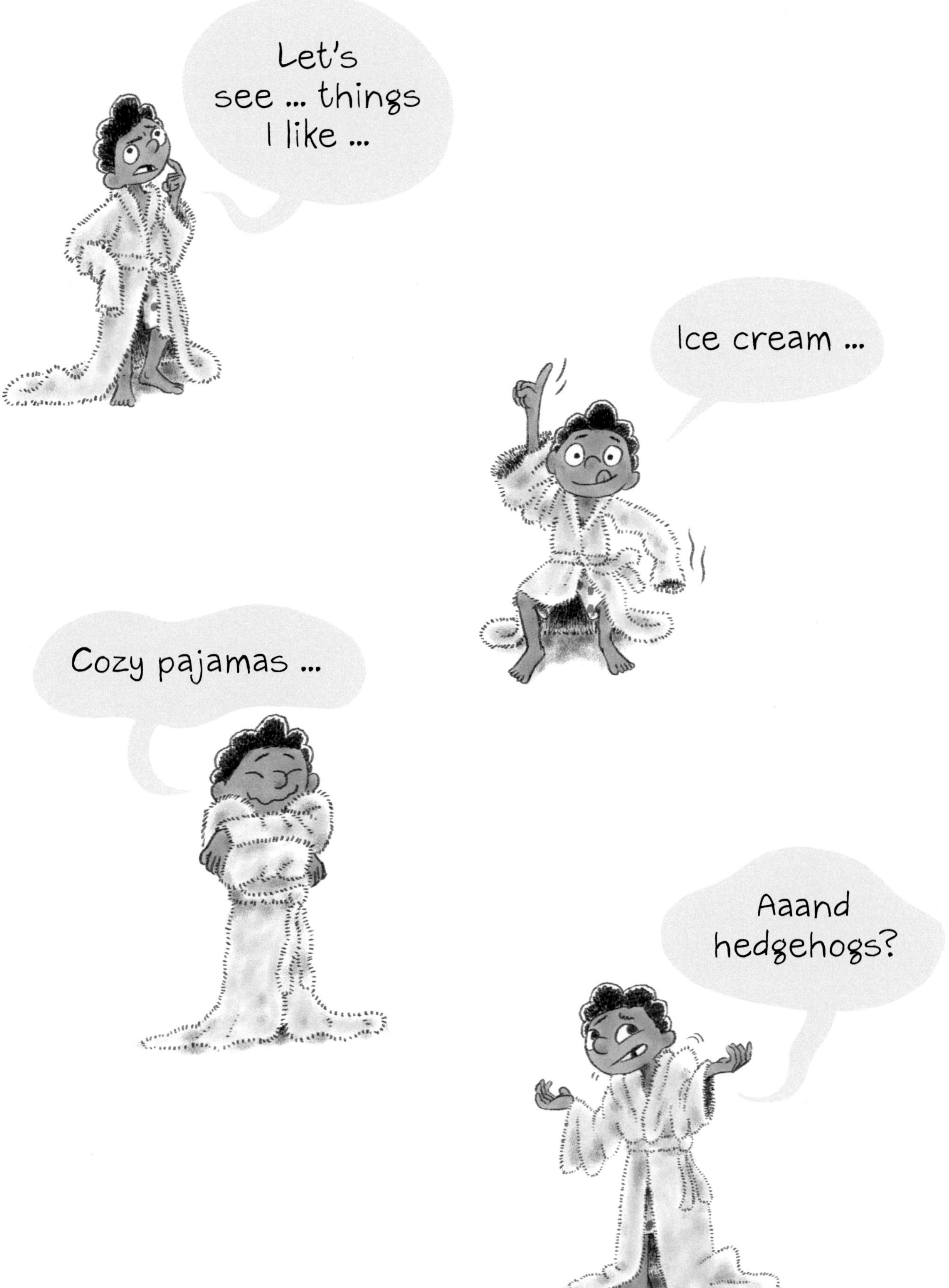
Let's see ... things I like ...
Ice cream ...
Cozy pajamas ...
Aaand hedgehogs?

Hmmm ... I think I have an idea!

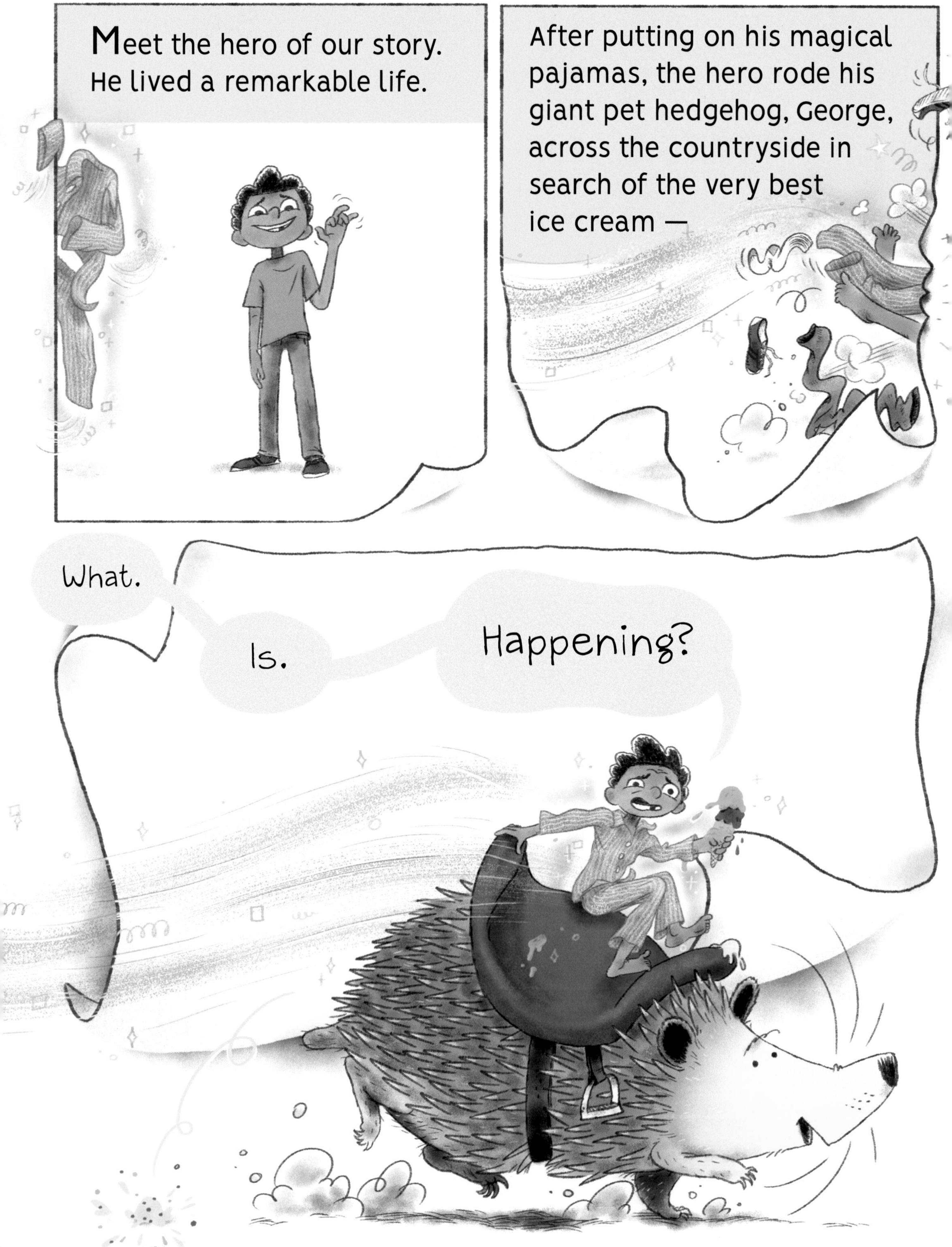
Meet the hero of our story. He lived a remarkable life.
After putting on his magical pajamas, the hero rode his giant pet hedgehog, George, across the countryside in search of the very best ice cream —
What.
Is.
Happening?

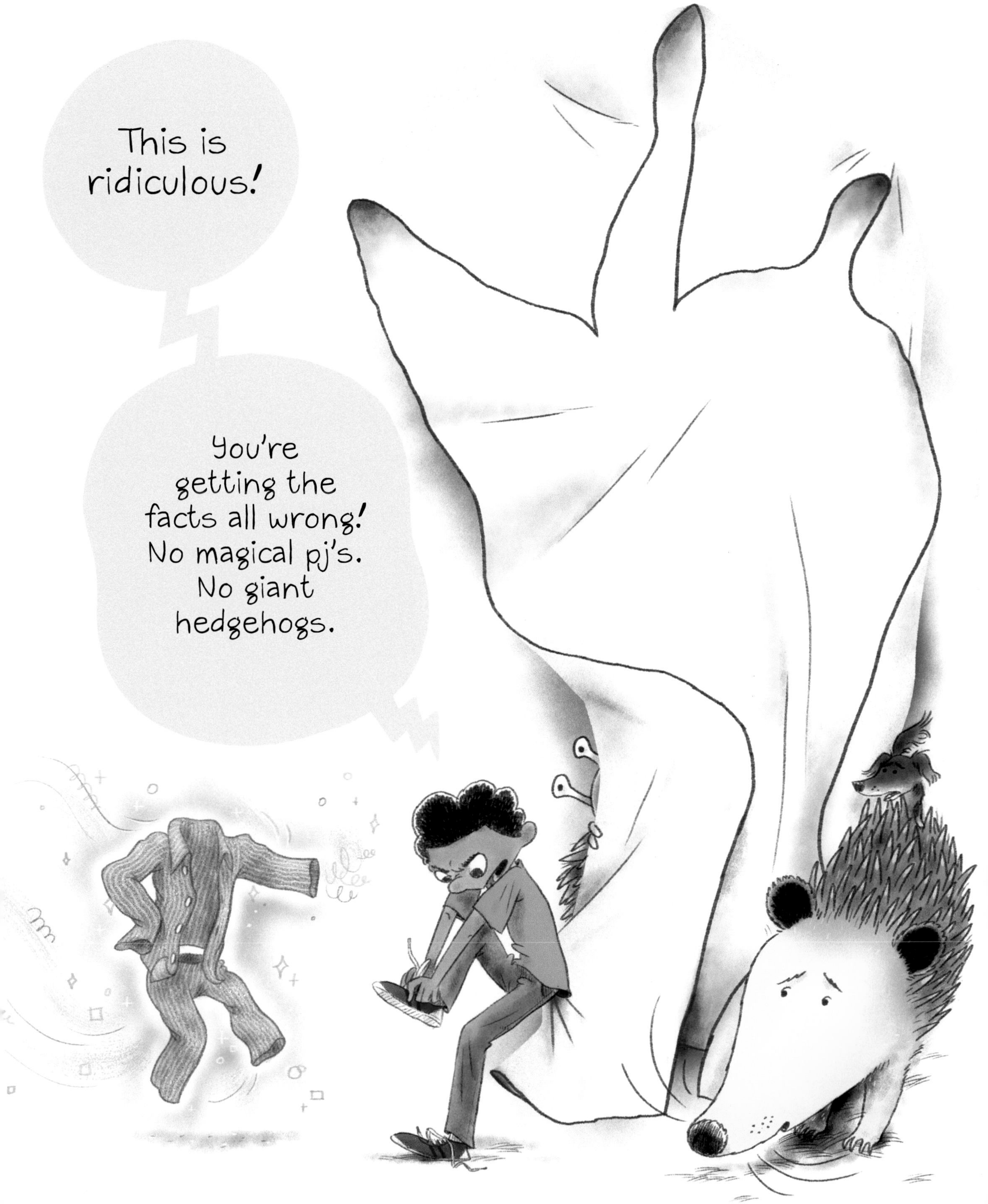
This is ridiculous!
You're getting the facts all wrong! No magical pj's. No giant hedgehogs.

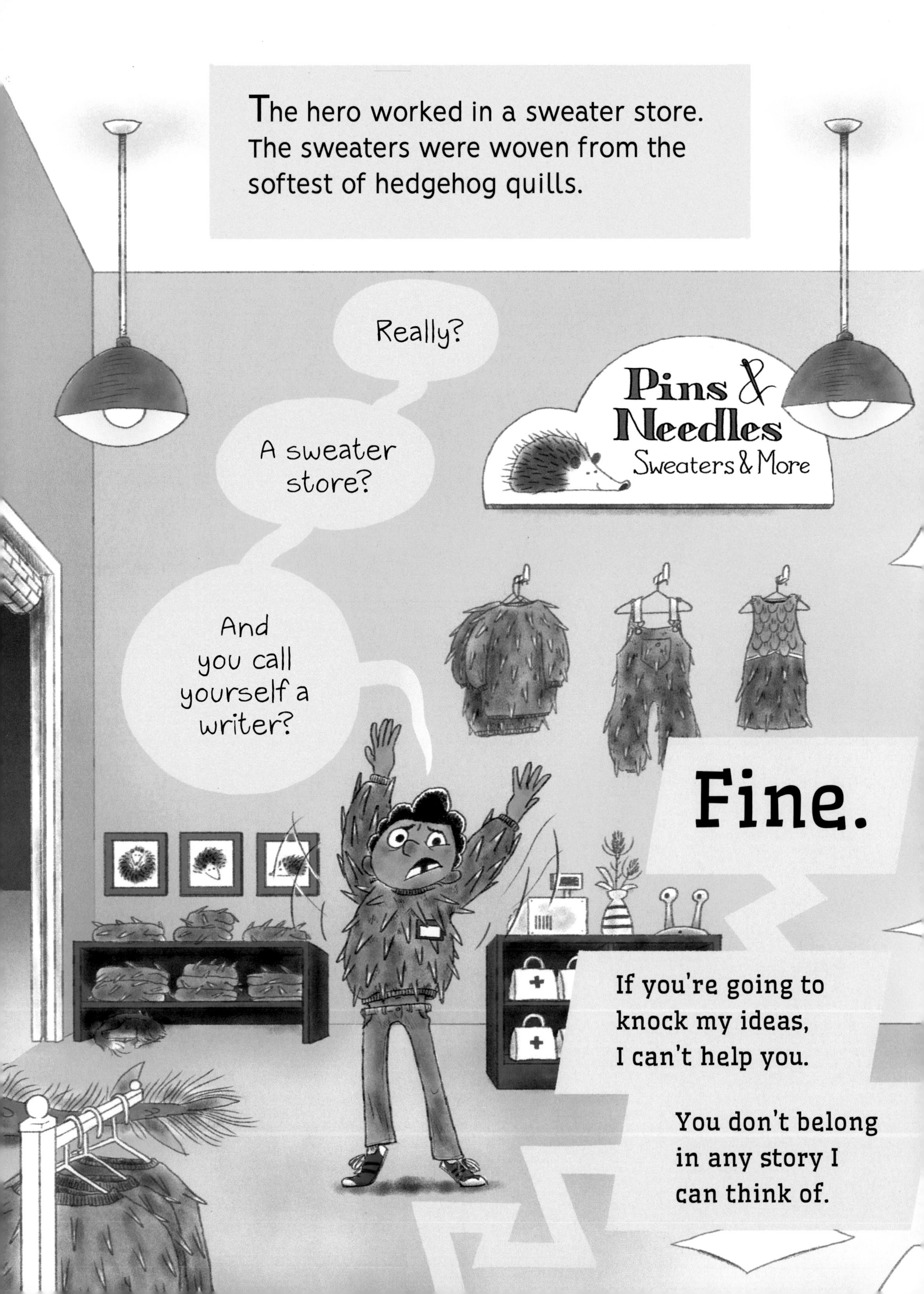
The hero worked in a sweater store. The sweaters were woven from the softest of hedgehog quills.
Really?
A sweater store?
And you call yourself a writer?
Pins & Needles Sweaters & More
Fine.
If you're going to knock my ideas, I can't help you.
You don't belong in any story I can think of.

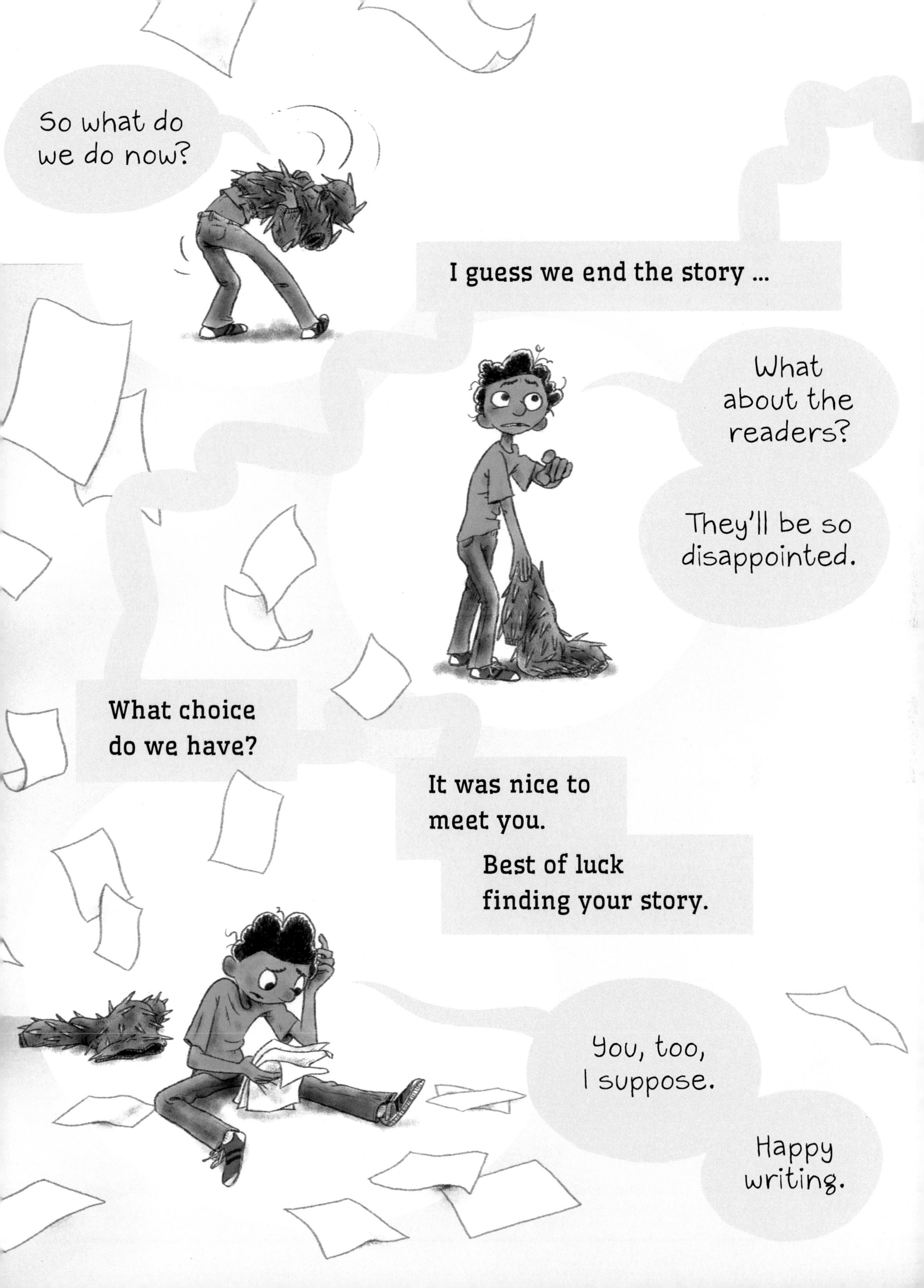
So what do we do now?
I guess we end the story ...
What about the readers?
They'll be so disappointed.
What choice do we have?
It was nice to meet you.
Best of luck finding your story.
You, too, I suppose.
Happy writing.

THE

WAIT!!

END

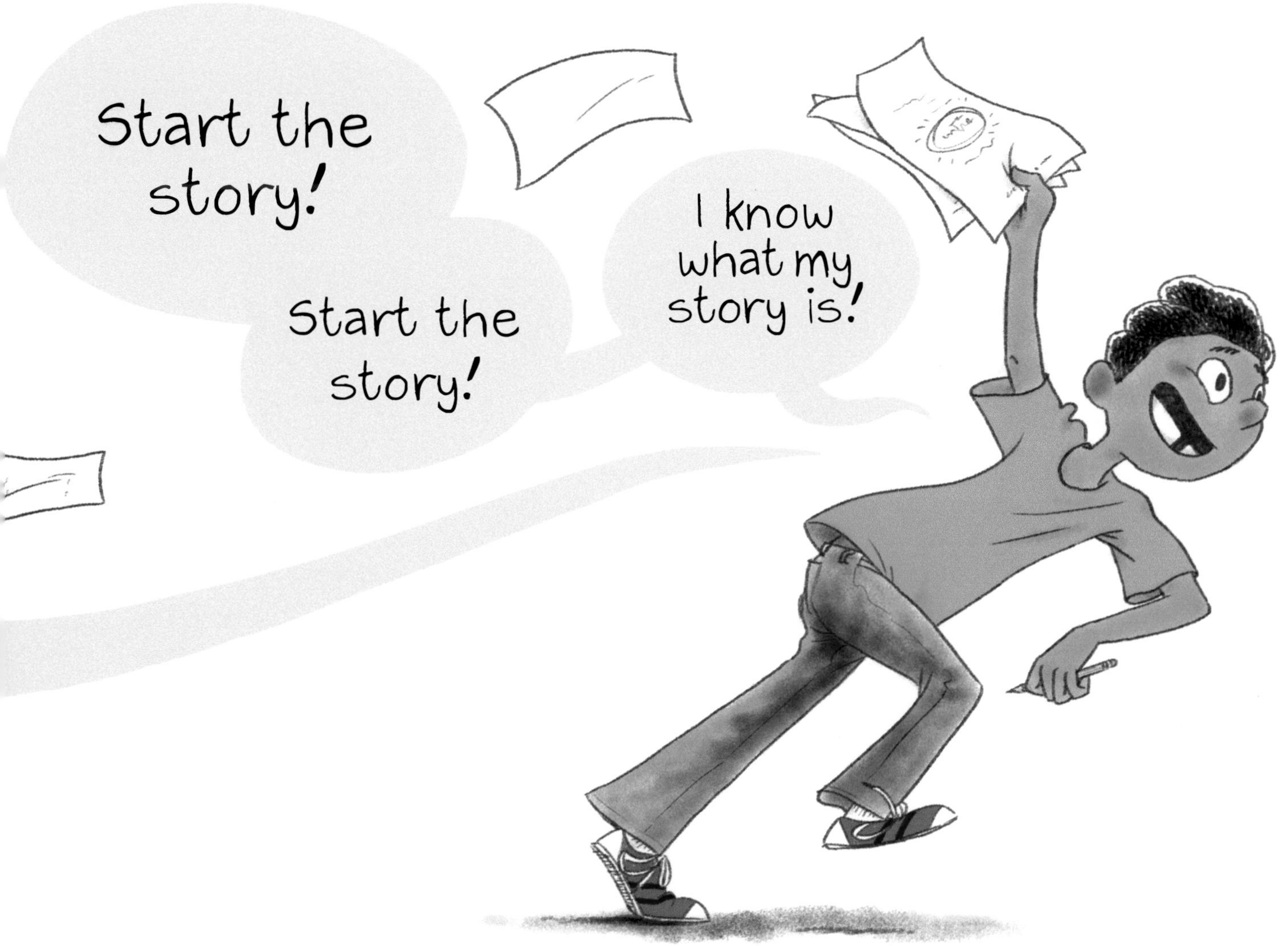
Start the story!
Start the story!
I know what my story is!

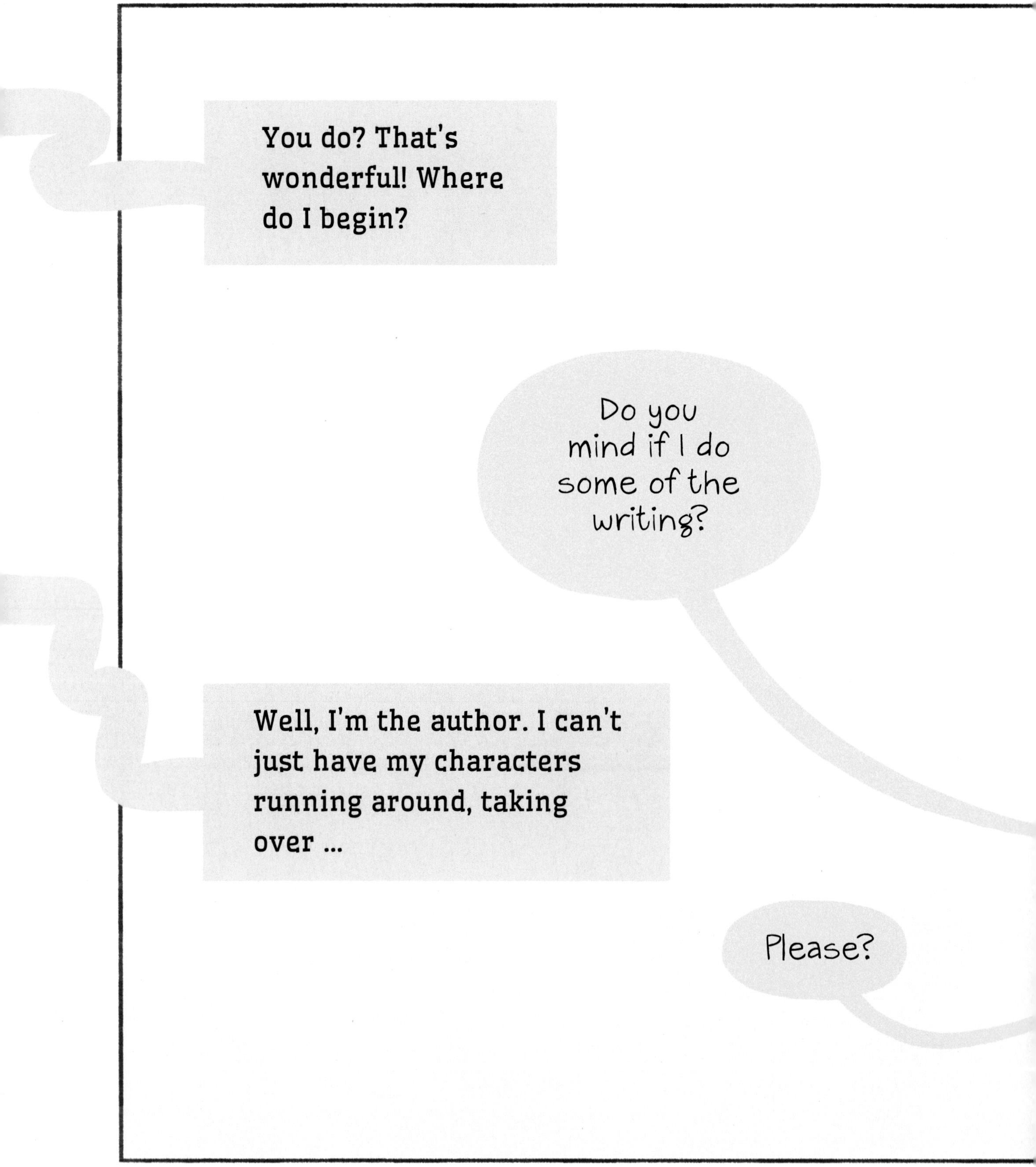
You do? That's wonderful! Where do I begin?
Do you mind if I do some of the writing?
Well, I'm the author. I can't just have my characters running around, taking over ...
Please?

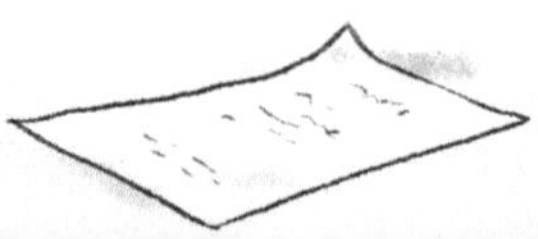

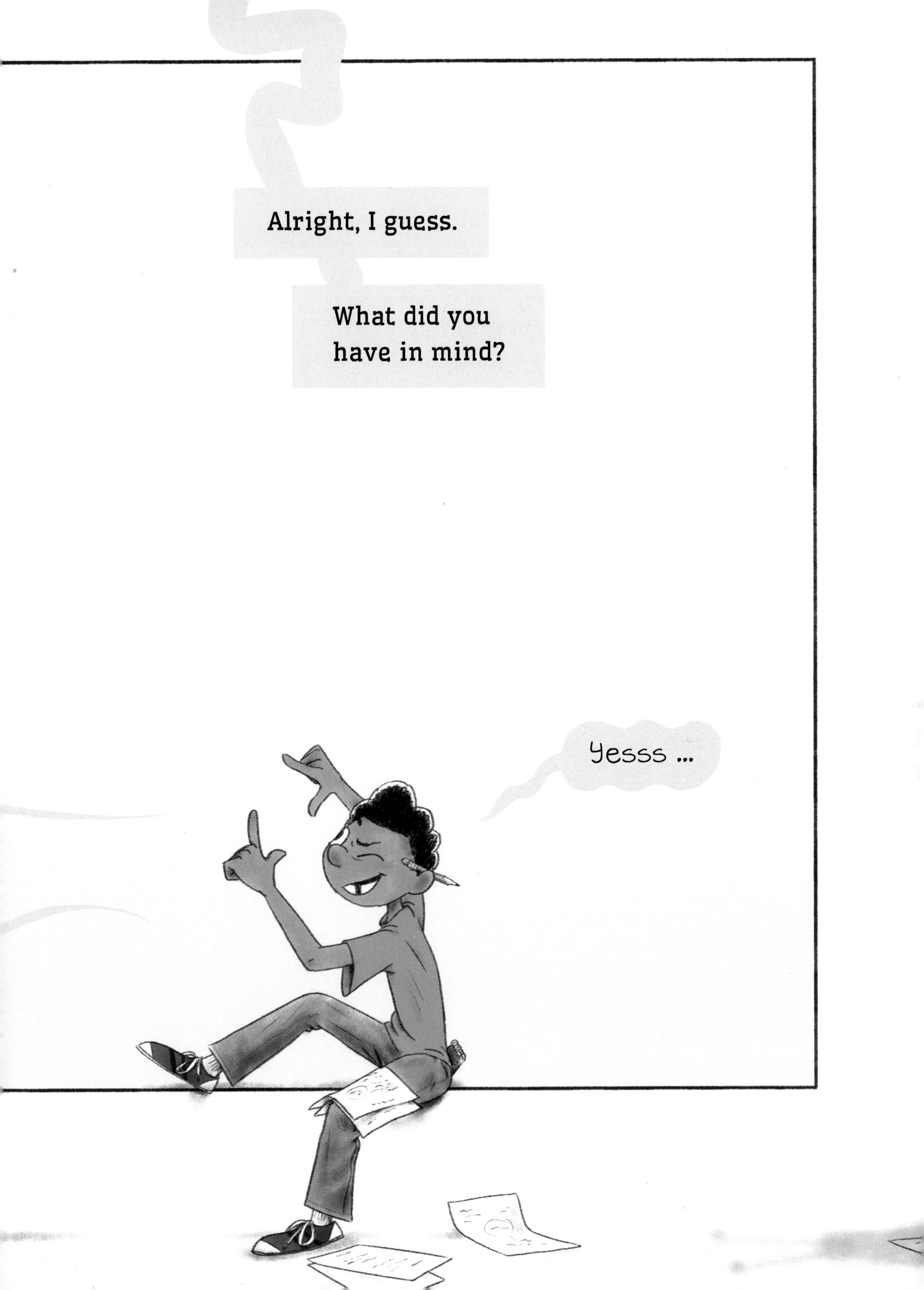
Alright, I guess.
What did you have in mind?
Yesss ...

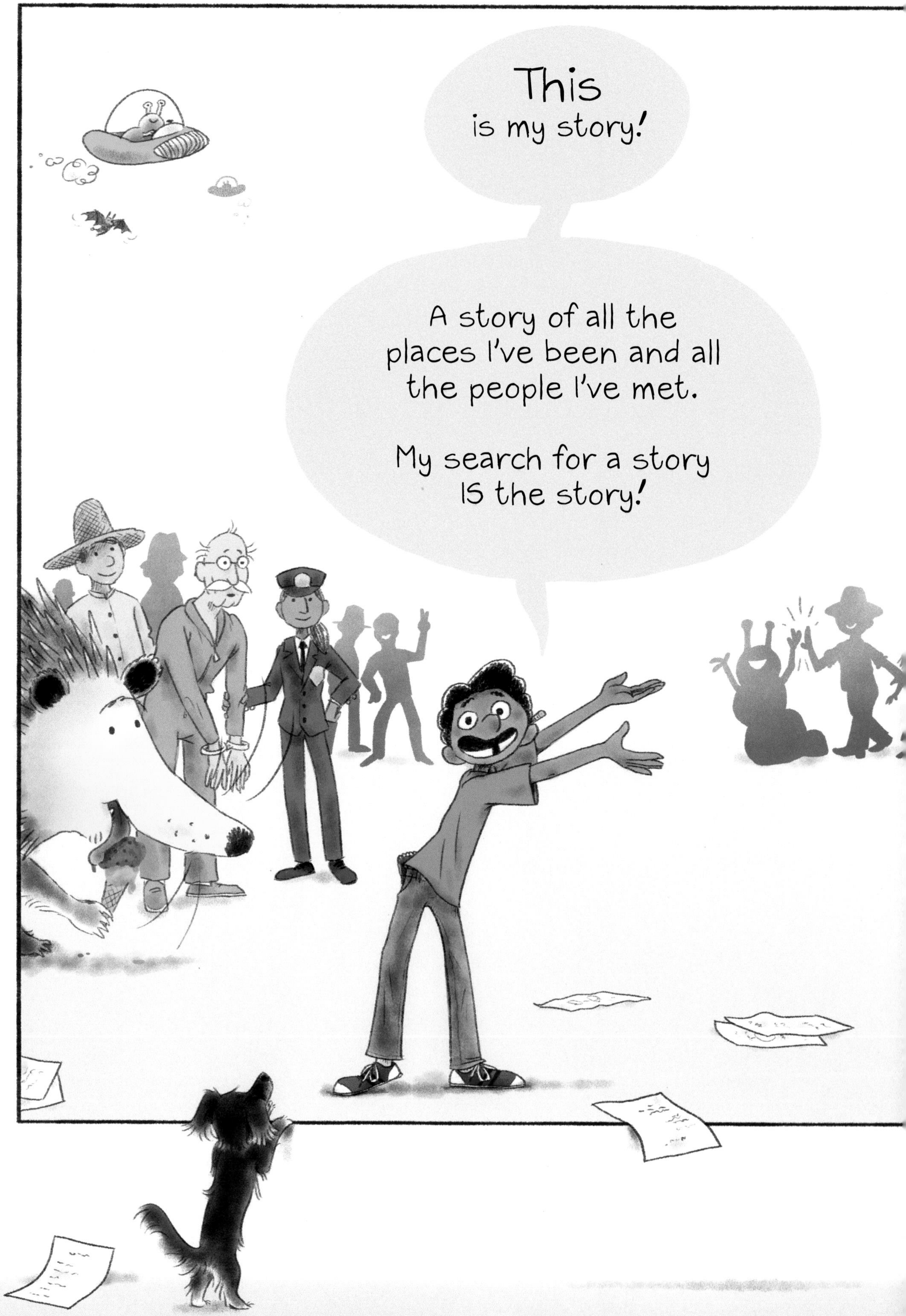
This is my story!
A story of all the places I've been and all the people I've met.
My search for a story IS the story!

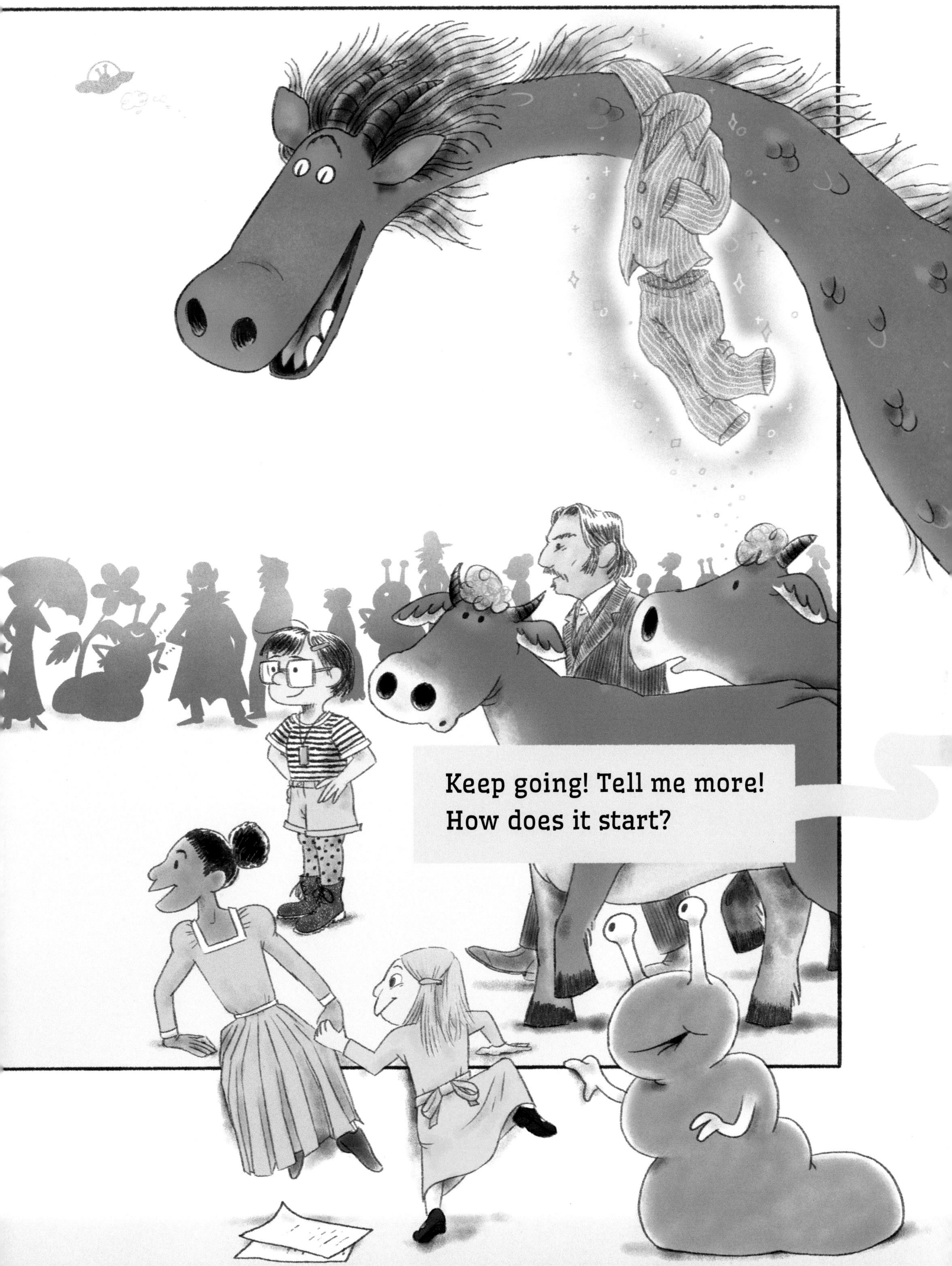
Keep going! Tell me more!
How does it start?

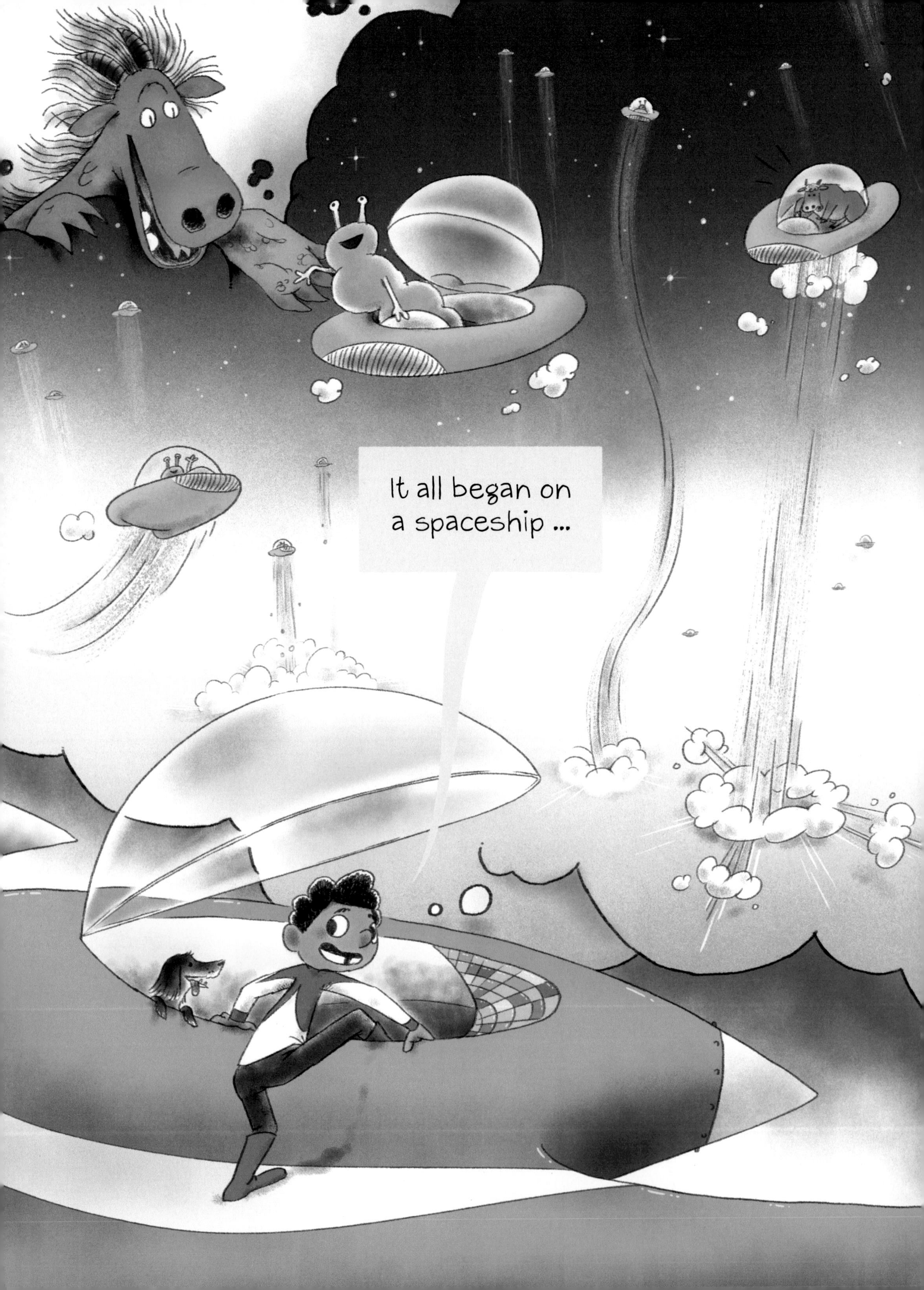
It all began on a spaceship ...

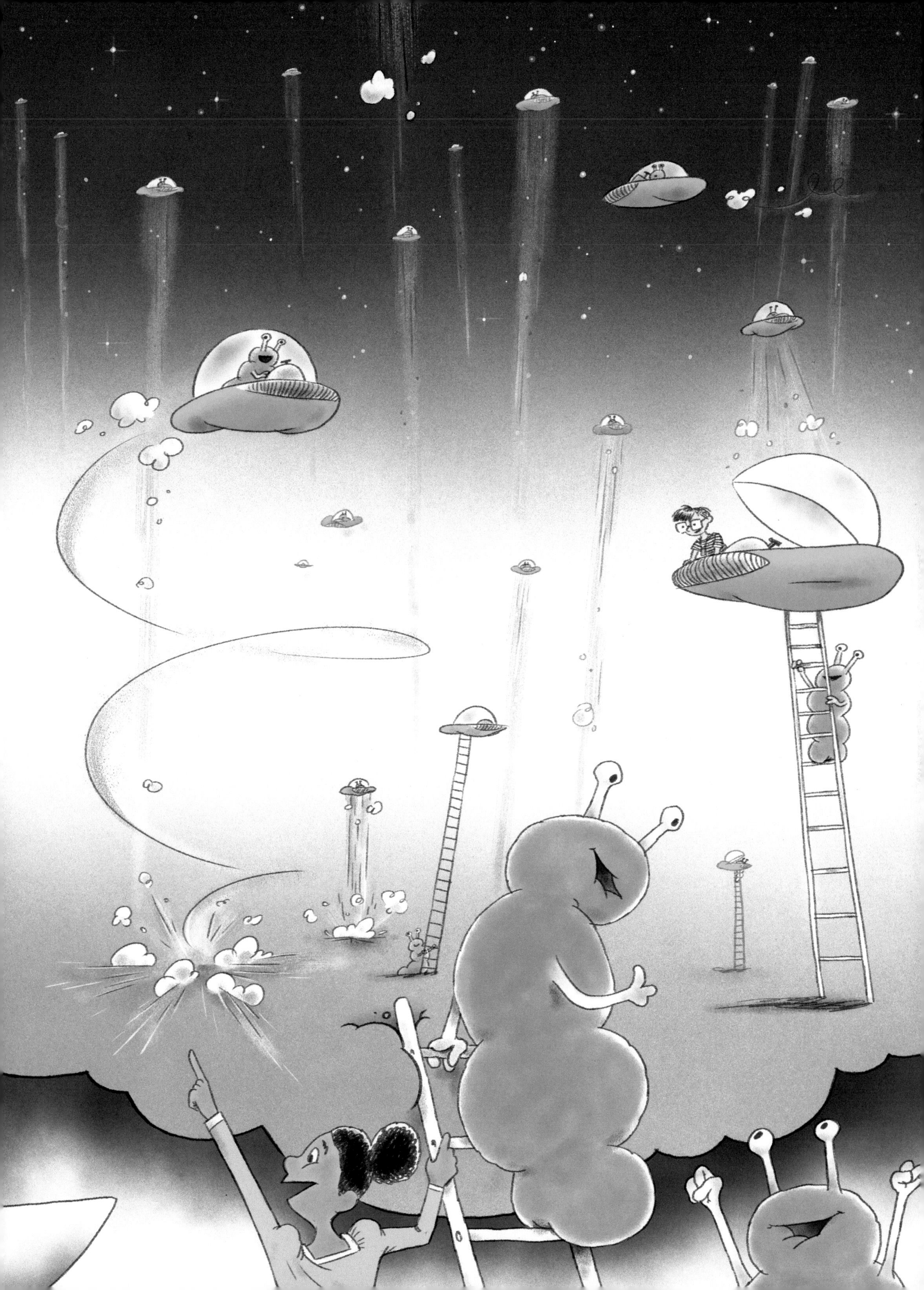

Hello, reader!
It's the author here. Pleasure to meet you!

The hero in the story you just read tried out many different kinds of stories, or genres, before finding one he liked. Before you go, I thought I'd share some of these genres with you. Knowing about them might help you decide what kind of story you'd like to read — or even write! — next!

FICTION stories are made up of imaginary people and imaginary events ... and sometimes even imaginary places! There are lots of different types of fiction genres to choose from:

· **Realistic fiction** takes place in a believable setting — like your home or school — with stories and characters similar to those in real life.

· **Historical fiction** is a made-up story that takes place sometime in history, like ancient Egypt or the Old West.

· **Fantasy** stories are completely unreal. They often take place in a made-up place, while the characters can be absolutely anything you can dream up.

· **Traditional literature** is made up of fairy tales, folktales and myths. These types of stories have usually been passed down from generations long ago and often include lessons for children.

· **Mystery** stories often have a detective solving a crime or investigating an unusual situation. Sometimes these stories are called "whodunits."

· **Science fiction** usually takes place in the future and can be full of futuristic technology and made-up science. It often features aliens!

NONFICTION is based on facts and is meant to share real-life stories and knowledge:

· **Informational nonfiction** is written to inform readers about a specific topic. It can be about history, science, art — or anything at all!

· A **biography** is a person's entire life story, written by someone else.

· An **autobiography** is an author's own life story.

· A **memoir** is an author's account of a specific time or event in their life.

POETRY expresses ideas and emotions in an imaginative way. It is an interplay of words and rhythm and sometimes rhyme.

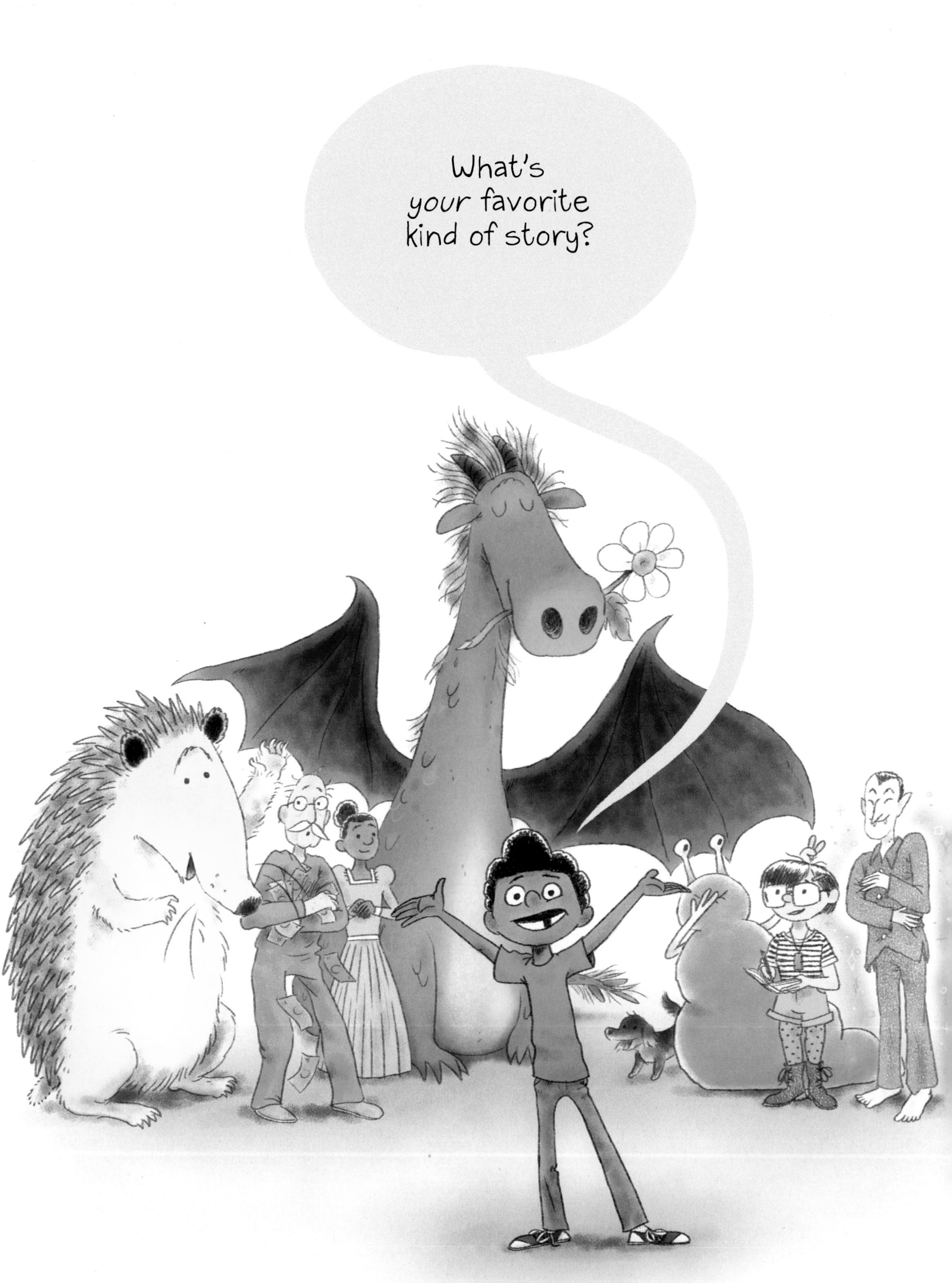
What's *your* favorite kind of story?